12 Days Of Chri

12 Days
Of
Christmas
2016

Burdizzo Books

12 Days Of Christmas 2016

Copyright Matthew Cash Burdizzo Books 2017

Edited by Matthew Cash, Burdizzo Books
All rights reserved. No part of this book may be reproduced in any form or by any means, except by inclusion of brief quotations in a review, without permission in writing from the publisher. Each author retains copyright of their own individual story.

This book is a work of fiction. The characters and situations in this book are imaginary. No resemblance is intended between these characters and any persons, living, dead, or undead.

This book is sold subject to the condition that it shall not, by way of trade or otherwise, be lent, resold, hired out or otherwise circulated without the publisher's prior consent in any form or binding or cover other than that in which it is published and without similar condition including this condition being imposed on the subsequent purchaser

Published in Great Britain in 2017 by Matthew Cash, Burdizzo Books Walsall, UK

12 Days Of Christmas 2016

CONTENTS

Twelve Drummers Drumming - Calum Chalmers 5

Eleven Pipers Piping - Anthony Cowin 21

Eleven Pipers Piping #2 - Matthew Cash 35

Ten Lords Leaping - Edward Breen 51

Nine Ladies Dancing - Daryl Lewis Duncan 71

Eight Maids Milking - C.L. Raven 97

Seven Swans Swimming - Matthew Cash 113

Six Geese Laying- Ezekiel Jacobs 141

Five Gold Rings - Betty Breen 167

Four Calling Birds – Jessica McHugh 185

Three French Hens - Mark Leney And Forbes King 209

Two Turtle Doves - Calum Chalmers 227

A Partridge In A Pear Tree - Matthew Cash 253

12 Days Of Christmas 2016

Author Biographies
275

12 Days Of Christmas 2016

Twelve Drummers Drumming - Calum Chalmers

MAKING A DRUM IS a time honoured art; it takes time to prepare the skin to make it just right for drum leather. No matter how skilful you are at skinning a beast there will always be fleshy lumps that will require removing, you have to almost caress the hide with a sharp blade to delicately shave of the meaty parts. It takes time, but it becomes rhythmical, soothing as your blade slices through the flesh, peeling it back in small chunks to reveal the treasure skin beneath.

Then you need to soak the flesh for 2 weeks in a pot of diluted lime, this softens the hairs allowing you to gently shave the skin to create a smooth layer. I love this part, all those tiny little hairs rolling up, hairs you could hardly see soon become little tumbleweeds flicking across the floor.

Now you need to remove the epidermis from the hide, again you turn to your sharp blade and scrape at it. Personally I don't do this part for long; I resort to a fine sandpaper which I use to massage every inch of the skin. Getting your hands so close to your craft has an almost euphoric feeling, the little clouds of dust swirl majestically as you breathe heavily across it.

I then use oak bark to tan the hide. It's beautiful how I can hunt in the same woods that produce my bark, it is as if the trees themselves give me their skin to help me perfect mine. Such a majestic offering compared to the fight that ensues when I find my prey.

The skin now soaks for 9 months. I have vats of oak water throughout my basement allowing me to remove the skin every 4 weeks and give it some fresh barky water; this also means I can start a new hide every 4 weeks. It's a process, a structure which allows me to produce my craft quickly and efficiently. I love it.

Now this is the most exhausting part, the currying. I have to hang the skin taut in a wooden frame, and allow it to dry slightly. Before it is too dry I have to rub a smooth, rounded stick across its surface. The motion slowly stretches the skin giving it that perfect smooth feel, that soft tender leather that you just want to run through your palms. This has to be done until the leather is dry so stopping is not an option, and with me being on my own I can't take it in turns. At first it was exhausting and I would ruin a few hides. But now, now I have it down to a perfection, I can sleak the hide all day. That's what it's called, the rubbing of the hide is called sleaking; aren't you glad I'm here to tell you these things.

Part of my own unique process is to now smoke the hide; I use cherry wood. I have tried a few types but cherry just seems to work best, plus the smell is amazing. I would almost swear that it even gives the hide a rich reddish tinge. To keep this colouring I rub in an oil and give it one final sleaking. Look I know it's weird but I have to do this part naked, there is something so primal about feeling the oil and the leather against your skin, the idea that the two fleshes are united in this final process.

I'm not a pervert or anything, seriously it's not like this gets me hard or anything, it's just about getting back to nature. Don't fucking judge me, don't look at me with those pathetic judging eyes! I don't need them looking at me, I can just pluck them, out I don't need your face, too many fucking holes anyway.

I crack him across the jaw with my sleaking pole, even with his mouth stuffed full of rags I can hear the regret in his groans. Blood dribbles down from his bottom lip gathering in his beard. I raise the pole causing him to flinch, he knows now.

I don't want to hurt you I need you to understand that, I need you to realise that you are precious to me, I'm telling you my secret, telling you something I hold very dear to me.

He stopped crying long ago, I'm not sure if I broke him or if he's just all cried out. Either way his puffy red eyes stare at me blinking rapidly. I put my hand softly on his thigh triggering him to pull away, gently but purposely I grip him tighter and pull his leg back before me. My fingers twirl on his flesh, minute hairs on his bare skin dance with my fingertips as I push them aside.

I've found that the key thing with hair removal is you have to do it after you do your skinning, if you do it before then the razor, no matter how sharp, scratches the surface. You never get that smooth feeling back, your fingers can feel the indentations as you run your hands across. It distorts the sound of the drum, fractures the sound as it reverberates across the surface; you never get that crisp sound back.

Sweat trickles down into his crotch, beads of cold, salty perspiration gather and run stream like down his thigh. He watches me with precision as I trail the flow with my finger, my eyes transfixed on the beauty of the turbulent flow meandering over his skin, hairs altering its path causing new and unpredictable changes.

The one thing you have to remember, and this is where most people mess up, drums can't have holes in them, that is obvious, but skin, skin has holes in it, a belly button, an anus, these things have to be noted when planning the skin. Holes are a pain, especially when it comes to your choice of kill tactic.

My first time I used a gun, it was messy, it was stupid. The bullet tore right through the abdomen, the best fucking part!

The doorbell above me rung, I spent so much time in the basement nowadays I really should install a speaker down here.

One moment please. I bellow skywards.

I check the ties on his wrists, ankles and gag. I need his silence.

Standing on my porch stood a friendly face, Andrew Slater had been a customer for many years now. He ran a music shop across town and swore blind that my drums were the best he had ever heard, he was selling them faster than I could make them and had a waiting list going into triple figures. Andrew was making a killing from my drums and would often slip in an extra £100 into my payment, I always argued with him but every now and then he would win.

I made these drums for love not money, I knew they were good and I knew there was always going to be a market, I just wanted enough to get by. I had no need for trinkets and toys, I had my drums.

Andrew flicked a finger in acknowledgement as I emerged from the basement door, locking it behind me. As I opened the front door Andrew offered a slight chuckle.

'One day you'll forget to lock that door and I'll finally get to see your secret process'

'If you did that I'd have to kill you' I winked back at him.

'No doubt brother!'

Andrew had been pestering me over my process; he had even offered me a 50% stake in his shop if I parted with my secret but my lips remained sealed, I was very particular with whom I parted my secret to.

Offering him a beer he accepted before sitting heavily on my sofa, in front of him sat my new batch of drums ready for his shop.

'Always 12′ he remarked tilting the neck of his beer at the display.

'12 per hide, that's all I can get, anymore and I'd have to start making smaller drums'

Sitting in the rocking chair opposite I dusted the crumbs from the table beside me before putting my beer on the worn surface.

A beam of sunlight split through the room, dust spiralling through the spectacle like sweat on skin, the same turbulent flows of unpredictability briefly mesmerizing me.

'So Lewis, are we going to argue again or are you going to take the extra cash from me today?'

'I'm no charity case Andrew; I have my life just how I want it'

Andrew forced a laugh 'Jesus Lewis I know that! But here I am getting rich from all your hard work. I could double what I'm charging and people would still be willing to wait years for your drums. I just want to make sure you don't feel hard done by'

Picking up my beer I gripped my bottle tightly; envisioning smashing it across his face, shards of green glass embedding into his cheek as I rained down blow after blow onto his crimson face. He must have sensed my hostility, throwing his arms skywards he backed down.

'Ok ok I know when I'm beat, I won't be the good guy and give you more money for your labour but I do want to know one thing…'

He watched me with a sly grin.

'Whatcha do with the dicks?' He erupted with laughter at his own joke; I couldn't help but join in.

'You're assuming they are all male' for some reason this just made us laugh more.

I didn't have any friends, Andrew was my closest thing to one, I suppose I kept the prices low to keep sales high and keep his visits constant. Being around him kept me sane.

12 Days Of Christmas 2016

I waited until the sound of Andrews car became comfortably distant before locking the front door and heading back into the basement. Our conversations always fire me up to start creating a new batch of drums.

I ignore my guest and head to this month's soaking drum, the leather should now be ready for sleaking. Dipping my hands into the cold and dark liquid I caress the skin under the water, I love this moment, the moment just before the reveal. I almost want to remain in limbo, not knowing the quality, floating in a high of anticipation. I can't hold myself back anymore and my hands slowly pull out the leather, brown water cascading down each fold.

The skin was perfect, the colouring, the feel, everything was just right. I squealed in delight. I get to do this once a month and it was worth every second I waited for it.

Clipping it above my head I stepped back to admire my work, sleaking would have to start tomorrow, I was going to have to leave it in the drum for another 24hrs but I just had to show off the true beauty of it.

I move aside to show my handiwork to my guest, his swollen eyes squinting in the dim light as he tried to focus. I scurry over; I had to let him feel this leather, to truly appreciate it he had to feel it, he had to let it drape over his flesh. I drag his chair towards the skin, tricky considering he was throwing himself about so much.

Placing him directly under the leather I lift the legs and drape them, one either side of his neck, I hold them close to his face, rub them to let him experience the true perfection.

His eyes bulged, pure terror seeped from his pores the sweat rubbing into the leather. If only he understood how long this took, how many nights I had spent creating something so perfect. No matter how much I tell them they never understand.

I whip the leather away from him, he didn't deserve to appreciate this, I tried to be nice, I always try to be nice and they never fucking appreciate it! I slam the back legs of his chair down, hoping that the vibrations rattle his bones. Moving around to face him I hold his face and wipe the tears from his cheeks sucking them from my fingers, tasting the salt.

'If only you understood, if only you could see how long this process takes me!'

Through the slits of his puffed up face I could see his wide pupils dancing frantically, it was always the same, it was if they thought they could tear themselves free with rapid eye movement.

'Shhhh' I whisper into his ear, stroking his hair, holding him close as I try to reassure him. I hadn't finished my story from before, he must still be curious as to how he was chosen, how rude of me!

12 Days Of Christmas 2016

…My first time, my first kill with a gun, was wrong, it destroyed too much skin, I was left with only enough to make 6 drums, only half my usual. It didn't help that I had used a shotgun rather than a rifle. Looking back at it I still can't believe how stupid I was! What was I honestly expecting to happen?

At that point I decided against all guns, I only carried my handgun for my own protection but any gun used to hunt with was just too risky. I wasn't a fantastic shot which meant I always had to aim for the abdomen, the most valuable part. Fine when you want meat but useless for leather.

I dabbled with a bow and arrow and found that I had fantastic upper body strength, I could fire an arrow deep into a tree but again my aim was terrible and ended with too many missed opportunities.

Then it dawned on me, the head, the face, they had too many holes, it was useless to me. Whatever I did needed to be done at close range and to the head. It felt so primal, so natural to be sneaking up against my prey, one swift hit and then it was mine. A silent and deadly act, it was perfect.

My hand patted at the wound to the back of his head, he no longer winced at my touch, he was beginning to understand my cause.

And you, you came to me like an angel, my little black angel, your skin is going to be perfect, the pinnacle of my work. Imagine the drums, imagine your leather pulled taught over the drums, your leather so dark it pulls the light in and holds it, traps it.

He remained resolute, his eyes transfixed on the skin hanging before him, he was admiring my work, finally he was understanding the sacrifice for my art.

He leant forwards, as if trying to reach the skin once more, his eyes now full with an acceptance that this is his destiny. I was proud of him, he had come so far, from being a screaming man curled up on the floor to this, this beautiful expression of true art.

I ran my hands down his arm until I reached his restraints. I knew it was a risk but I could feel the want coursing through his veins. Each thump of his heartbeat remained steady and strong. As I unclipped him he calmly moved his hands onto his lap, he waited patiently as I released his head. Lulling forward it was apparent he was weak but something deep inside pushed him forward.

Finally I came to his ankles, dried blood crusted around the shackles, an open wound seeping fresh blood. I took my time, ensuring that they were released with as little discomfort as possible. As the heavy metal crashed to the floor he stood up.

I stepped back allowing him to walk towards the skin; something inaudible escaped his cracked lips, his mouth moving slowly as if to say a silent prayer. I move in behind him to hold him, to embrace him during this beautiful moment. My head lulls against his arm, my hands gripping his waist lightly.

Suddenly his elbow whips back.

The bastard! The absolute scummy fucking bastard!

I wipe the blood from my lip, my nose still steadily producing more. The light from the basement door at the top of the stairs flickers as he unlocks and flees through the front.

I act quickly, I gather my handgun from the kitchen drawer and head out in pursuit, he hasn't got far, I could see his sleek body just inside the woodland. I fire a warning shot to make my point but it makes no difference, he continues his escape.

Before long I am hot on his heels, his naked body no match for the thorns and brambles these woods produce. I can hear him crying out in pain as branches snap across his torso.

Then it hit me, the thorns, the branches, they will all be slicing his perfect skin!

Please stop! I Scream, please, you mustn't damage your skin it needs to be perfect!

He continues his getaway.

I beg him; plead him to be more considerate, I could feel the emotion boiling up from inside, my eyes clouding with tears. Every thwack of every branch causes me to wince. Blood splattered up against the surrounding trees, bloody footprints smeared into leaf litter.

I want to stop, if I stop then maybe he will too, but if I'm wrong then he will leave forever, taking his beautiful hide with him.

Please, don't do this to me, I continue to beg.

I fire another warning shot but for this one I take my time and aim a little closer to him, a little too close, the bullet detonates a sapling to his side, he flinches and turns back to face me. I can see only fear in his eyes, he wants to escape, he wants to leave. The bastard betrayed me!

I scream at the top of my lungs, a truly bestial howl of betrayal. The Gods themselves would want to intervene to put halt to this tortured cry.

My prayer was answered, a few feet before me he trips and stumbles into a small ravine, too fixated on me he must have stopped paying attention to the trees around him. As he falls a protruding branch tears into his naked flesh. Blood dripped from the leaves, frayed chunks of skin lay at his side, sitting, cowered against a mossy outcrop he cups his wound. Every inch of him was bleeding; his entire body was shredded beyond use.

Why? I begged, why would you destroy something so beautiful? Why would you stop me from making you perfect?

He sat almost silently, his chest heaving, laboured with each painful breath. Blood was bubbling from his chest, a small piece of wood nestled deep into his lung.

Kneeling before him I began to cry, I was so close to reaching perfection, so close to helping him achieve his purpose, but it was all for nothing.

Whatever the Gods had planned for me this was not the path I was meant to take, this was never meant to be. Perhaps this was their way of saying the skin wasn't good enough, perhaps another skin is meant to be my 'Mona Lisa', my 'Sistine Chapel', my masterpiece.

No, this was my masterpiece, this skin was mine and the bastard took it from me. I alone failed to persuade him, I was to blame.

Beating the ground I sobbed and wailed, my drum skin man watching, unflinching.

Why the fuck did you run? Why didn't you fucking understand what I was doing? I was helping you, I was going to make your skin immortal!

Hours passed; all the while he just sat there, silently watching me. It was dark before I realised he was dead.

He left me again, left me all alone.

12 Days Of Christmas 2016

Eleven Pipers Piping - Anthony Cowin

ENGINE STEAM BILLOWED PAST the dirty windows of our carriage before rising into the low-hung clouds like transient ghosts. Above us a skein of migrating pipers cut through the wisps of haze in the sky. Below them, through the murky glass, I saw clusters of small houses tucked into the embankment, each rooftop creaked under the weight of snow. The hills behind resembled salt mountains where children climbed with sledges, dogs yapping alongside them on their descent. Every snowflake is fragile and unique they say. Yet soon enough those pallid angels whitewash the landscape concealing the darkness and dirt.

It was then in my meditation of light and darkness I caught the menacing eyes of a figure shifting between the ghostly snowmen dotted across the hills. The creature meandered through the snow like black ink spilt across a fresh ledger. I shivered. Not from the frosty draught hissing through the many fissures around the doors and windows of the ageing coach, but from the icy claws that scraped down my spine. I'd had enough of spooks and chills to last a lifetime. Crystal Hall had seen to that. I closed my eyes to vanish any spectre observing from the hills and pictured my daughter Isabella waiting for my return.

I was eager for the calamitous week to end and greet the new century. The Twentieth offered so much hope. My cousin informed me in a letter home from the Transvaal that mankind grew tired of war and I agreed with his sentiment. Peace would soon be upon us. Mankind had grown from adolescence, ready to dress in the tailored suits of adulthood.

That Christmas Eve brought no peace to my mind, however. It was an evening of misfortune that punctuated a dreadful week making me yearn for home more than I'd appreciated. I feared the prospect of the railway even on calm days, but the violent snowstorm that had swept across the country that morning made stone of my heart. I'd debated returning to Crystal Hall, even with the fears I held of the old house. Though whether my terror was at the prospect of encountering the foreboding Lady Hayward or one of the shades rumoured to lurk in the corridors, I couldn't decide. Though I still held a set of keys for the lodge there. Even though I'd depleted the remaining hearth wood, it would still be preferable to the hopper huts where one could hire a cot per night. I had enjoyed using the lodge to undertake my business, a warm setting for the overwhelming paperwork a large house such as Crystal

Hall requires. But Christmas Eve was upon us and my family expected me home back in London.

Though I had to admit, the dread of meeting one of the alleged ghosts that roamed the Hall and its grounds helped me to decide upon the train journey. I had encountered a spectre just the once and in the company of servants. A fact that set my mind to believe after the event it was a clever practical joke fashioned by the staff to unnerve new visitors. A trick with candlelight in front of a mirror, perhaps. Unlike many of my peers my interest in the macabre extended no farther than fireside tales and never in the pursuit of evidence. I even dispelled the accounts of sandpipers crashing through windows in Crystal Hall as a portent of death. Concluding it a simple disturbance in their migratory patterns. A mere coincidence that a handful had shattered against the stained glass of the Hall's chapel the week prior to Lord Hayward's demise. Or that family records disclosed a pair of the birds had met a similar fate the morning of master Hayward's drowning a decade previous. My academic mind refused to attribute any dark forewarning to these events.

Seated next to me on my homeward passage was a porcelain doll that regarded my travelling companion with dead blue eyes. Eyes that clicked open and closed through golden lockets of hair as the train rode over uneven rails. The gentleman opposite didn't notice her blinking. He was asleep underneath his lowered hat, his face sunk into a mink collar. Yet I envied that coat which lent him the appearance of a hibernating bear, an accessory very much out of place inside the third-class carriages. He snored out mists of breath from beneath his cover and save for the rhythmic heaving of his chest he was as still as the doll. I resigned myself to a carriage void of distraction, as neither companion, bear nor doll, offered conversation to pass the hours on our way to London. Yet I took comfort in counting out the man's breath and turn of the wheels. Each a marker toward my destination where I could gift the porcelain figure to my daughter.

The doll had not been my first choice for my Isabella; a stunning music box had captured my eye and imagination earlier in the week. It was a jewel amongst a crowd of wax and porcelain dolls in the window display in the village toy shop. I made it my business to disturb the fresh fallen snow every day after lunch at the inn and pass that window to stop a moment or two. There I would look upon its splendour. I realised soon enough that hot stew and warm ale were preferable to the plate of cold cuts and weak tea served at Crystal Hall.

That walnut music box with winter rose inlays weaving around the front and sides was small enough to fit a child's hands. Inside, amongst the blue velvet lining stood a frozen couple joined by holding hands. The pair sprang into life skating around a miniature spruce in the heart of the box, forever circling, with the turn of a silver key.

I gasped when I saw the ticket. The price just short of a fortnight's wage. I had been absent from my family for three months, my visits home sparse, so I threw caution into the country gale and make the purchase. Each day I wished to see the pair dance, to listen to the music, to see them come alive. It became an obsession. My final Friday at Crystal Hall could not arrive soon enough.

When the day arrived, I snatched my salary from Mr Sunday's hand and sprinted to the toyshop. The couple skated around the tree to the faint chiming of Silent Night drifting through the frosty circles in the window when I arrived. Had they known I was coming?

How my heart broke when the shopkeeper's hands reached forth and lifted the delightful toy from the display. He wrapped the music box and invoice in brown paper with a tie of string. A familiar looking gent dressed in full black attire tipped his top hat, took the parcel and left.

My gaze followed him as he walked across the square to the tearooms, the small doorbell ringing out my misfortune as he disappeared.

I recognised the man from the London train, a first-class passenger. I had often envied him, travelling in such luxury whilst I rode in the cramped and smoky carriages.

12 Days Of Christmas 2016

Some men it seems have it all. I shook the snow from the rim of my bowler and entered the toyshop.

I accepted fate and purchased a member of the audience of dolls from the window display, the dancing couple's routine now lost to them. Although Isabella would never know of the musical skaters that knowledge hung over me like a canopy of failure. Maybe it was homesickness or the burden of work I had endured at Crystal Hall those past months. It could have been the cruel and bitter winter in the stark landscapes of the countryside. But like the rooftops, I also felt a weight upon me, not of snow but of guilt.

I surveyed the doll as it sat on the carriage seat next to me, its cream complexion flourished with two rosy apple cheeks. A pretty thing, though it made my heart despondent. Each time I considered its glassy blue eyes I felt one more drop of weight fall upon me. I turned to gaze out of the window, now iced with a forest of leaves etched into the glass. A tiny bird smashed against the frozen fauna, warm blood streaking down the pane melting the frost. Then, before I could catch my breath from the shock it happened a second and third time in quick succession. The last sandpiper breaking the glass and falling into the carriage. It flapped its broken wings on the seat next to me, pinhole eyes closing as it gave up its ghost. Red streaks cast onto the doll's porcelain face.

12 Days Of Christmas 2016

Before I had time to remove the bird and clean the toy, an almighty clamour from outside shattered my thoughts.

The carriage came to a halt. I heard shouting through the screeching of wheels and whistles. A group of men congregated at the roadside debating a young lad's terrible report. I made it my business to join them to see if they were in need of assistance. I let the bear continue his sleep, for the odour of brandy had become obvious in his misty breath. The night air hit me as I stepped from the coach. I looked back daring myself to wrestle away the man's coat from his shoulders. The doll's eyes seared me, sapphire flames inside the darkness of the carriage. I shivered, once again from something that crossed my grave more than the effect of thin winter air. I let him sleep and strode to the band of men trying to ascertain the reason for the holdup.

It was a disaster. The earlier London bound train had derailed as it entered a tunnel through a snow-covered mountain. We dashed down the hills to the railway line guided by swinging orange lanterns, with prayers and dread filling our hearts.

Hell had broken through to Earth concealed inside the blizzard. Fires blazed inside a fortress of smoke, bodies lay strewn across the snowy embankments. These fires were not the warm crackle and glow of the hearth. This was the furnace of death. The smell of burning flesh drifted past before returning with each heave of the wind. Screams echoed through the valley, alien noises I wish never to experience again. It wasn't just fear in those howls, but dread and realisation of a true horror.

I set about pulling bodies from the upturned carriages. The local men were so industrious working with only lamplight and the radiance of the burning train. We dragged out corpses through the night, the hope of finding even a solitary survivor from the wreck faded with every hour that passed. Pools of thawing ice dampened our pursuit. Our tears dropped into the slush. The cold reality of death chilled every man. It was evocative of the landscape of war and it convinced me more than ever that our taste for battle was an insanity.

The night disappeared.

A silhouette of a man stood atop of the hill surveying the wreckage, the Christmas morning sun rising behind him. It was the same black figure I'd witnessed stalking the snow-covered hills earlier. His dark rapier of a body slashed through the crystallised slopes. As soon as I caught a glimpse of him, he turned away and vanished into the haze like a phantom. Several snowmen had melted from the heat of the wreck and now resembled white hillocks dotted with black coal scars.

I sat on the frozen ground, the snow around me melting as if skulking away in shame. I have no humiliation in reporting I wept for those unfortunate beings, not a survivor amongst them. The clamour of the horror stifled the world. It was as though a bell jar had lowered over the Earth where I sat.

Then I heard it, slow and faint but unmistakable, a miracle in the wilderness of despair. Copper tines scraped 'Silent Night' through the muffled chaos of cries and splintering wood. I fell to my knees digging into the snow beside the roof of the upturned first class carriage. I must have resembled a stray mutt scavenging for buried bones long since forgotten by other hounds. My flesh sensed pain for the first time in hours as I struck something firm, something colder than the grave of crystals that surrounded the wreck. I brushed away the ice and the wet mush of parcel paper to expose the music box; the unfortunate gift now rested in my hands.

A scalded face exposed by the melting snow seemed to rise from the ground. I scampered backwards, digging my heels into the wet ground, a scream caught in a cloud of mist around my lips. When I stopped, I looked down at the music box clasped in my hands.

A tear dropped from my eye and splashed across the wooden lid, crystallising as soon as it fell

I remained kneeling in the snow listening to its chiming lament for a while. Then the music stopped. I looked around now conscious of my actions. I dared to look at the corpse at last.

The black clothes tattered, his face burnt beyond recognition. I covered the gentleman's face with his charred top hat, wrapped the music box inside my coat and raced back to my carriage. The track cleared enough to allow our train to pass with a slow and careful motion. I sat back in my seat and slept the rest of the journey. I never noticed my bear of a travelling companion was absent from the carriage. No doubt moved to a more comfortable carriage of the train befitting his standing. The doll remained. Drained and exhausted I slept.

I awoke from a nightmare to see the black figure sitting opposite, his top hat lowered like the bear man's. He raised his head to greet me, his scaled face stabbed an icicle into my heart. It was an echo of my dream. I was alone inside a cab close to my home. We approached the elm-lined street in London where I called home for the final part of my journey. The horse hooves muted on the blanket of snow. The river a short distance away glimmered under a full moon. I thought of the stories of people using the frozen Thames as a rink in the past and smiled. I clutched the walnut box and thought of the miniature couple waiting to do the same. The horses stopped with a pull of leather. I paid the driver, home at last.

A hot bath and a glass of brandy helped me thaw. Thereafter the rest of the Christmas evening was full of excitement and joy. The events I had witnessed still preyed upon my mind, but my family brought such happiness like coals in the hearth of my thawing heart. It was good to be home. Good to be with the people I loved after witnessing such horrors that very morning.

I paid respect to the souls of the perished within my grace and thanked the Lord for defending my life. For if his guiding hand had not prevented my connection with that train I too would be one of those broken bodies on those tracks covered in sheets of calico. The discovery of a misplaced ledger at Crystal Hall had saved my life. Those added hours of bookkeeping made me miss a train that never found its destination.

Saved me from a grave of crystals.

Then I saw him again outside the window that dark spectre who stalked me. Had he followed me from the countryside to Camden? Why would he do such a thing? Then the thin air of the country paid me a visit as my blood froze at a new thought. What if he was a spectre from Crystal Hall?

I thought of the music box hidden in a desk drawer in my study, wrapped in yellow paper for Isabella. No matter what I tried the thing no longer came to life, the couple frozen for eternity in a muted world. Was it a coincidence, the silence of the chimes, they stillness of the dancers? The spectre's head turned toward me with a ghoulish grin. If the night outside had not been so bleak, I'd have sworn he had no face at all and wore a mask of half scalded flesh for effect. I pulled the drapes to keep the phantom from sight. A train whistle screamed in the distance.

I observed my daughter who sat through dinner with her new friend at her side. When I had pushed her chair into the table, she had whispered it was the greatest gift she had ever received. How she loved that porcelain doll, its eyes now appearing azure with warmth. It made me realise that I must do it. I made plans to leave after we had eaten. Begging my wife's forgiveness, I promised to be swift. I'd been away so long another hour was little in comparison.

Save for a handful of well-wishers who braved the climate and the skating rink of streets I found London deserted. I took the invoice from my pocket and checked the address. It was a treacherous walk, but I turned up my collars and proceeded.

The maid hesitated to disturb the widow at first, but after a time a black figure glided from the shadows toward the door. Her ashen face shone like the moon in a grey winter sky. I tried to explain my imposition and to offer my condolences, but words failed me.

Then from the stairwell a small figure appeared. It was a girl the same age as my darling Isabella. She rubbed her eyes as she strolled to the doorstep, wrapping her little arms around her mother's legs and leant into her hip. I felt foolish to be disturbing the family during this time of anguish.

I held out the parcel which the child took from my hands and unwrapped with glee. Her tired eyes widened and her face illuminated as she lifted the lid. At once, the couple skated around the Christmas tree to the chiming sounds of the carol. Her mother's eyes filled with tears though not of grief, but of hope. She gazed at her daughter and the realisation arrived. She was a widow, but a mother also and such a gift was her child. Darkness lifted from her expression. I wondered if she had noticed the dancing man's features transform as he skated around that miniature tree as I had? His expression of gloom transformed into joy. The resemblance to the dead man and his striking wife was startling. I wondered for a moment if that was the reason he'd purchased the toy. The similarity offered him more right to own the thing. Yet those skaters had never looked as they did in the dim lamplight cast from the widow's doorstep. I'd observed their dance every day through that small toy shop window, the faces I had seen were maladroit caricatures of young lovers. But here as Christmas night passed away I watched milk white angels skate inside that box. I retreated down the steps to the accompaniment of Silent Night fading behind me.

A solitary snowflake fell from the heavens and landed on my lips like a cold kiss. Many more fell around me as I walked through the barren streets; my only company was the echoing bells of St. Paul's cathedral and a solitary piper sang in the distance. When I reached my own house, the dark spectre stood waiting. However, he appeared less sinister. He tipped his hat to reveal a face that offered me a warm smile emerging from the charred flesh. The smile of the male skater. The smile of a loving father and husband. Then he disappeared in a swirl of snowflakes, his laughter fading inside a coiling wind that whistled like a far-off locomotive. Snowflakes melted into the lustre of his black coat.

Later I lay in my bed drifting to sleep in the warmth of my home with my family close a thought occurred to me; some men indeed do have it all. Outside the inky sky turned white as many more snowflakes fell. I reflected once more how each flake was unique and all were so fragile, so easily they can disappear, unless they stick together.

12 Days Of Christmas 2016

Eleven Pipers Piping #2 - Matthew Cash

WHEN I FIRST SAW the ad in the Daily Record I thought, "Fuck me they desperate for an audience or what?"

The Edinburgh Royal Military Tattoo, the traditional annual extravaganza that sucked tourists from all corners of the world like a weathered old pisshead draining the glass for the last few dregs of cheap shitey lager.

Be proud of your country, that's what the advert said, like we weren't already. I fucking love Scotland me. I guess they wanted more of us natives going to one of the country's largest events rather than millions of people from around the world.

I usually just watch the show on the BBC whilst having a carry out and a bevvy. But this year I found myself filling out the wee competition form in the newspaper and sending it off. It was free post and all.

Well, the days wound on and on, posters began to be slapped up everywhere advertising the Fringe festival which usually coincided with the Tattoo. The showmen from some of the more zany acts featuring would cruise the Royal Mile in their fancy garb telling all and sundry to flock to their shows.

It was a good time of the year, I didn't mind the tourists, brought some culture to the place, and last year I pulled a couple of yank lassies that came in my local so it wasn't too bad for me.

Anyways, I put it down to drink, drugs, too much cheese before bedtime, the usual suspects, but for a few weeks after filling out that wee form I started having weird dreams.

Now, I hadn't really been to the castle since I was a nipper. My dad took us just before he took himself off to England with some scuzzy yo-yo knickered floozy. But, being a resident of this fine city meant it was always up there looking down at us. The castle is bloody impressive, sitting up there scowling down at the city, acting the hard man up on its mountainous pedestal.

So even though I hadn't been up there since I was a laddie I was up there again in the first of these recurring dreams.

It was night time and I was standing at one of the walls next to one of them big cannon jobbies, the ones they use to fire at one o'clock each day. I was taking in the view of the city at night, the lights, the monument protruding like a space rocket out of a Giger painting, and it was fucking beautiful. That was when I heard bagpipes, not so strange I hear you say, being in Scotland's finest city and all, but it took me by surprise. It sounded funny, distorted like. I turned and wandered the ground to find the source. It didn't take me long, I mean bagpipes aren't exactly your most inconspicuous musical instrument. The castle was deserted, something I thought odd, I thought places like these would be secured twenty-four seven, but nonetheless I walked towards the source of the cacophony. As I got closer I could see the piper standing on one of the walls, his back to me, the pipes tucked under his left arm. I was impressed but not too surprised, Scotland the brave and all that, to see him standing up there without any safety harnesses or anything above what is probably a several hundred feet drop. I may have over or underestimated that measurement but I don't really care, I'm no mathematician, it was a long way down, enough to make you go from man to jam in under a minute.

I noticed there was something weird about him, fanning out behind the back of his head was a spray of something, a semi-transparent headdress, like when you see fashion models with stuff sticking out of their hair, feathers and stuff.

Whether it was the moon poking out from behind a cloud or just some convenient dream coincidence, a dim glow illuminated him showing me his fucked up tiara. It was the whacking great glistening hole in the back of his head that gave it away. A headshot bullet wound in suspended animation. The spray at the back, shards of skull, matted clumps of hair, chunks of brain, blood splatter frozen like red jewels, crimson pearls, molten wax seals with a bullet's stamp. All the time he played the damn pipes oblivious to this, surely fatal, head wound. I recognised the tune. Scotland the brave.

Obviously I'm a rational man, it was a trick, a marketing ploy for one of the festival acts, a costume. I leant against the wall and checked out his front. They had done a really good job, made him look like he'd been in a car crash or something. He was blackened and red. His fancy clothes melded to his skin, the front of his kilt had been burnt away and there was just a mess of gore from his chest downwards, he wore his entrails like a shrivelled tatty leather apron.

"Awesome costume brother." I shouted up at him, he ignored me, not even a wink, but then again he didn't look like he had any eyes. One was just a blood filled hole and the other a crisp black cavern.

It's weird, even though I could see no one other than the lone piper all around me the deafening cries of thousands of people woke me from my dream.

Turns out it was my clock radio alarm playing some upbeat hip hop bullshit to get me the hell out of bed. I always made sure I tuned it into the most annoying radio station so as to piss me off from the get set and get me out of bed.

I punched the bastard which was on the other side of the room, and novelty, designed like a punchbag, and shuffled through to the kitchen. That was when I saw the letter on the mat.

I picked it up frowning like I'd never seen a bloody thing before, and slit it open with my thumb. A posh embossed ticket to the Edinburgh Military Tattoo. "Fuck me," I thought, I'd never won a thing in my whole life, even in sports at school the only thing I managed to catch was athletes foot in the changing rooms. I was stoked man, really stoked. There was nothing else in the envelope aside from a brief compliments card. It made me happy but I think I've already said that, so even though the date was still a few weeks away I went out after breakfast and bought myself a new shirt.

The big day came and I splashed out a bit on a few drams of quality whisky from one of the posher places on the Mile, I thought why not man, it wasn't every day people like me got to go anywhere nice.

I found a nice restaurant, had a blinding steak and chips, you could tell it was posh nosh, Gordon Blue or whatever the fuck it's called, because the dinner came on a chopping board and the chips had the skins on still. It was lush, especially with the whisky afterwards.

12 Days Of Christmas 2016

When I left the place I walked up the Mile, up Castle Hill towards, well, the castle. Hundreds of people were already flocking in that direction, groups from every corner of the globe, a hive of activity with the buzz of dozens of different languages. Made a change from the only person being unintelligible I came into contact with being Fred the jakey from outside the bookies, I can tell you. It was nice, different.

The seating in the Esplanade had undergone a big change a few years back but I couldn't tell the difference, looked the same as it did on the fucking telly only obviously way bigger.

I was shown to my seat by some young spirited usher and just sat there taking in the experience really.

Where I was sat was dead centre like, opposite the castle. Best seats in the house brother, not far from the front either.

I sat whilst the place filled up, probably maximum capacity, every seat seemed full to me anyway. A bunch of female backpacker types were sat next to me, I'd didn't know where they were from, they weren't that talkative to me, even when I said "hello", but whatever I wasn't going to let in shit in my shower if you know what I mean.

Finally the show started with hundreds of dancers from, I forget where they said now, Zimbabwe or something, and they did this cool tribal piece with yelling and drums.

After that there were some wee lassie dancers from Skye and the islands up north, really beautiful man.

The New Zealand fellas, the Maori is it? The natives came on with all their gear and did one of them mad dances they do at the rugby. A haka. Scary bastards but really cool too, I was close enough to see the wee veins in their heads pop up when they yelled. Awesome

Things started getting more traditional when the Scots Guard paraded with their brasses and pipes and tartan, that was more like it. They played a medley of all the great well-known songs, I hoped to Christ no one would try and be modern like that year they went and did that gangnam style dance, that had been fucking ridiculous.

It was halfway through their set , well I don't know that it was halfway obviously, just an estimation, two almighty fucking crashes that sounded like the Devil fucking farting came from each side of the arena and everything went white for a second.

I instinctively ducked into the footwell at my feet, as chaos surrounded me. My first thoughts were the obvious ones in this sick and depraved day and age. And it turns out I wasn't wrong. Terrorists.

12 Days Of Christmas 2016

Panic everywhere, people were screaming and clambering over the seating to flee the castle grounds. I risked a peep over the seat in front of me and wish to God I hadn't.

The seating up each side of the arena had bloody great holes blown in them like an asteroid had shot through the place. Debris from the blasts was everywhere, crowds on the sides of the blast zones writhed like maggots to get away from the fires that were dotted about the place. There were pieces of people everywhere, all over the Esplanade. A lot of the performers had taken the worst of the blast but those lucky to survive it were busy trying help their fallen comrades. It was a battle zone.

Then I saw the lone piper, way up at the undamaged part near the main castle. A voice boomed over the speakers, those that hadn't been destroyed. "Keep calm and head towards the piper."

The fellow was limping badly, one of his legs was red and ruined, and no one was paying attention to him even though he waved his arms and shouted. So he took up the bagpipes and began to play them. This poor heroic fucker played wonderfully, it was in his blood this beautiful, beautiful bastard. He had been on fire for fuck sake and there he was playing, trying to round up people from every nation like some beautiful bloody ginger Scottish Jesus.

People had cottoned on and slowly but surely the frantic multitudes began moving in his direction.

That was when another threat presented itself.

From out of the crowds came the sound of rapid gunfire and more screaming started.

People started rushing around and running back towards me, I spotted the gunman just before I threw myself back to the floor out of the way of trampling feet. Aside from generic t-shirt and jeans that was all I noticed about him.

More gunfire came from further down where the crowds were rushing from the piper back towards the main entrance.

I'm not a religious man, and as we still don't know the reason for this bloody massacre, but if this was for a holy cause then I would hate to meet the God that condoned this shit.

One of the young students who had been sat near me stood on the steps, looking for one of her friends probably. I yanked at her trouser leg for her to get down when a bullet whipped through the air, ruffled her hair and blew her brains out of her forehead. My scream was but a wank in the ocean compared to the hell-noise around me.

12 Days Of Christmas 2016

I hid, I cried, I feared for my stupid useless fucking life, as thousands of people were being mowed down by crazy bastards.

A break in gunfire.

That was when I heard the piper still playing, he was joined by others, a signal for people to still come their way, that together they would be stronger.

The gunfire recommenced and I just thought of my miserable existence and the people being killed all around me. I belonged with them. I was nothing.

Whilst I crouched there contemplating my existence one of the gunmen stood right beside me, a black machine gun in his hands, bullets showered the running people ahead of him, his face smiling as he shouted something in another language.

I got the bottle of whisky I stowed in my pocket, took the cap off and took a large swig. Might as well die with a belly full of whisky. Maybe the fumes on the breath of my dead body would mask the reek of the piss in my pants.

Then something took over me and I found myself leaping up and smashing the cunt over the head with the half filled bottle. He hadn't known what had hit him and the fear that he may get up again once he had fallen made me go a little bit crazy. I stomped on that fucker's head until there was nothing left.

I shook, I had not expected that, but a fighting part of me had been ignited, if I was going to be killed by one of these bastards I was sure going to try taking at least another one down first. I grabbed his gun and a spare magazine I saw protruding from his trouser pocket. I didn't know what the hell I was doing.

I crouched back down and peeked over the seats towards the gunfire. I made out at least three other gunmen at different positions, open firing on innocent people.

My heart was still rampant from beating the fella to death, I wasn't worried whether or not I'd be arrested or anything, I doubted that I'd last the following ten minutes.

I crawled along the footwell behind the row of seats over handbags and other belongings people had dropped in the melee. Every now and then I popped my head up to see what was happening down on the Esplanade. The crowds were rushing to a band of determined pipers and the surviving military men began to skirt around them fencing them in. They were trying to protect the people but all the marching ones had were empty decorative rifles with fixed bayonets. The gunmen cut a swathe through the people running towards what they thought was safety. I saw mothers, fathers, sisters, brothers, sons and daughters from all around the world being gunned down by these deluded heartless bastards.

A few other people, Japanese I think, had taken to hiding behind the seats like me and shrieked when they saw me crawling towards them with a bloody great gun. I motioned for them to stay put but they were just frightened. The father grabbed his wife and the two wee bairns and legged it down the steps away from me.

The gunman pacing this part of the arena swivelled his weapon towards them and I saw the two bairns' faces explode all over their parents before the spray of bullets obliterated their legs and they tumbled down onto the bodies of their dead children.

I ran at the bastard.

I've never fired a gun before, I mean I've played your video games and stuff but that's the most I've done. I wasn't expecting the kick it gave when I pointed it at the fucker and pulled the trigger. The thing buzzed in my hands and a series of red spots like blooming flowers dotted the man's white shirt and went up in the air as the force of the thing made me shake. I took my finger from the trigger and my arms felt numb.

I saw the other two signal towards me and one of them moved across the rows in my direction.

I continued towards the Esplanade with the intention of handing over the weapon to one of the soldiers, the brave bastards who were trying to keep the people safe. The bombs had blown great holes in the stands, stuff was dropping off the sides, I think some were actually people jumping. I could hear sirens over the screaming and the whir of approaching helicopters. I hoped to hell they would hurry up.

The gunman fired at me and I dropped to the floor, the bullets missed me by inches as they zipped past my ears and made mincemeat of the padding in the seats. I stuck the gun over the back of a chair, aimed it in his general direction and fired it once more. I risked looking hoping I had struck lucky. I hadn't, the fucker, now he had seen I was armed, decided to spend the last of his time picking off the defenseless.

The gunmen worked their way towards the crowd of people in the centre of the Esplanade where the pipers still played, and the wounded were dragged amongst the debris from the bombs. The soldiers stood firm and defiant, but there wasn't that many of them to protect that number of people. I remember thinking that if only they would all as a collective rush the gunmen they could take them down.

The gunmen laughed and shouted more gibberish as they stormed across the Esplanade, reloading from spare clips hidden about their clothing. A few of the brave soldiers did do as I had thought, a group of about four rushed towards the gunman nearest to them but the bastard cut them down in a heartbeat.

I had lost all self-concern then, I just ran down the steps towards the murderous bastards.

I was probably few hundred yards from them, people had started abandoning the crowd, trampling over one another, doing horrible horrific things just to try and save their own backs but to no avail.

Then one of the bastards turned on me.

I dropped to the floor but not before I felt something whack against my arm just above the elbow. I had been shot. It fucking hurt. I rolled across the littered ground, dead and injured people everywhere.

One of the soldiers had taken the opportunity to attack the gunman whilst his attention was on me. I cheered as I saw the guy thrust his bayonet straight through the bastard's back and saw the tip burst from his chest. The soldier pushed the gunman to the ground and was instantly decapitated by the remaining one's fire.

I picked up the gun and ran towards the last gunman.

He was being more careful with his shots, taking out all the soldiers until none were left.

I could hear and see the armies of police approaching the entrance but wondered how many more people would be slain before the gunman was either taken down or turned the gun on himself. The fucker started on the row of pipers who stood steadfast until the bullets tore them apart, the defiant warriors refused to buckle and surrender to their enemy. Scotland the brave, man. The gunman stopped to reload, I sped up seizing the moment. All that was left standing above the frightened crowd who wondered how many more bullets the man had left and whether it would be them or a loved one who would be taken, was the lone piper. The one from my fucking dreams. As I got closer I saw the poor fella was in a right state, burnt badly and barely standing but something in the poor bastard made him want to play his pipes until they inflated with his last breath and sung the notes of his dying.

"Scotland the brave." I screamed in a war cry as I ran towards the last gunman. This is it, I thought as he turned his weapon on me but his gun got stuck or something. I ploughed into him and as we went down his gun went off and the piper stopped, the bagpipes giving one last pathetic wheeze. "No," I cried and looked down at the laughing muttering bastard. He didn't care, he expected to die, was all part of the cunt's bigger plan, whether it be some deluded promise to some Creator, or just some brainwashed cult. There was no fear in the fucker's eyes at all. I was going to kill the bastard so fucking much.

I raised the hard butt of the gun above his head, his olive-skinned face covered in blood spatter and perspiration, smiling, nodding.

12 Days Of Christmas 2016

I used the weapon to pound the living shit out of the fucker's arms until they were nothing but rags on the dirt. I dragged the cunt by the ankles across the Esplanade, screaming, "Scotland the brave." I think I had gone a wee bit nuts then. People looked at me like I was a hero or something, I didn't feel like one. I past the lone piper, bullet wound in his left eye just like in my dream, and dragged the fucker towards the approaching police and medical crews. As we met I could hear the chanting of the people behind me spur me on even though the blood coming out of my arm was making me giddy.

Scotland the brave.

Scotland the brave.

Scotland the brave.

Ten Lords Leaping - Edward Breen

LUCKILY FOR BOBBY THE Bump—so called because he was the youngest member of the Good Old Boys—the focus of the dog's attention wasn't on him. The beast was snapping and barking at the Street Vassal that he and The Pits had captured. The dog was one of those "banned breeds" the news goes on about all the time and she belonged to The Pits.

'Heel, Veronica, there's a good girl,' The Pits said with a pronounced lisp turning "there's" into "there'th." Not that Bobby could imagine anyone ever ribbing The Pits about it. Bobby didn't think there was a person alive that had ever ribbed the man about anything. If they were alive, then they wouldn't be for long.

'What's your name?' Bobby asked. He was stuck with being the good cop, because there was no badder cop than The Pits.

The Vassal answered with a nervous, tittering laugh.

He'd heard Vassals were fucked up.

'Come on, fella. We just want to ask you some things, then we'll let you go. In the spirit of Christmas, right Pits?'

The Vassal they had captured wasn't just any corner boy. He sold drugs, yes, but it wasn't that they were interested in. At least not directly. He, like all the rest of those known as "Street Vassals", came from a town called Hambly: a sleepy but reasonably large fishing and shipping town in the south of England. Bobby had been given his orders: find out what was going down in Hambly. There had been talk of a takeover, the Good Old Boys were tired of the Hambly Vassals selling on their patch. Bobby wondered why they didn't stage a takeover years ago, he didn't see that there was much anyone could do to stop the Good Old Boys if they wanted to move in.

'Pits? As in The Pits?' the Vassal asked. They were the first words he had said since he was abducted.

'Yeah,' Bobby said. 'So, you gonna answer my questions?'

Again the Vassal laughed his annoying laugh. Bobby was sure he was hopped up on the stuff he had been selling. That would make getting the information tricky. Not impossible, though. He did have The Pits on his side after all. Bobby nodded to the tall skinny man with the dead eyes and he got to work.

It started off lightly, as Bobby saw it. The Pits calmly put pressure on the Vassal's forehead, tilting his head back. Then he pulled back the boy's top eyelid and with the other hand poured a couple of drops of chili sauce in.

On the bottle it had written "Naga Ghost Dragon sauce," so Bobby supposed it would be hot.

The effect was immediate. The Vassal screamed and tried to bring his hands up to rub his eye but the leather restraints held tight. He bucked and writhed, his eyes rolling back in his head, his lids blinking spastically. The screaming turned back into laughter soon enough, though. The Pits held his head back and did the same to the other eye. Again he screamed and spasmed and eventually turned back to his maniacal chuckling.

'Are you listening now?' Bobby asked.

The laughing stopped and the Vassal nodded. He was trying to open his eyes but thought better of it, apparently, and kept them closed.

'We heard something's going down in Hambly soon, something about the Lords?'

This set the Vassal off on another fit of the giggles, worse than before. His face turned from red to a shade of purple before they subsided this time. What he found so funny Bobby didn't know. He nodded to The Pits again and those empty eyes regarded the Vassal before deciding what to do. He turned to his small suitcase and took out what looked like a perfume bottle, one of those old glass ones that has a long tube coming from the top of it with a bulb at the end to squeeze.

'What the hell?' Bobby asked.

'Atomiser,' The Pits said.

('Atomither,' thought Bobby.)

He unstoppered the chili sauce bottle and poured some into the atomiser. Then calmly reassembled the perfume bottle before giving it a few test squirts in the Vassal's face, causing him to flinch. When The Pits was happy it was working he placed his hand over the Vassal's mouth and nose. He held it for so long, Bobby thought he was going to suffocate the boy. The Vassal took a huge breath when his nose was released, at the same time The Pits squirted the chili up his nostrils.

The Vassal immediately started coughing and choking and making a kind of whining sound through his nose. Eventually, to Bobby's amazement, he started laughing again. By the time he stopped this time his body was shaking and no sound was coming out. Bobby thought the boy was dead, his head just slumped on his chest. Then after far too long he took a deep wheezing breath.

'Tell us and we'll stop,' Bobby said.

The Vassal just nodded, he looked barely strong enough to do that.

'Good boy, tell us what's happening in Hambry, what are the Lords up to?'

Again Bobby thought the Vassal was dead. His head was up, eyes open, but he still looked dead. Bobby was just going to get The Pits to carry on when the Vassal's eyes seemed to snap back into focus. There was no white, just red, and the eyeballs themselves looked swollen and lumpy. But he showed no sign now of discomfort. Bobby saw madness in those eyes and something else, confidence?

'The Ten Lords are Leaping,' the Vassal screamed. 'The Ten Lords are Leaping, the Ten Lords are Leaping…'

On and on the Vassal said this, laughing all the time until he couldn't say it for the laughter. Then he was shrieking so that Bobby wasn't sure if he was laughing or crying, he was sure he heard pleading amongst the cackles. Blood started pouring from his eyes and nose, that shade of purple came back to his face and he was bucking on the chair. Then it all stopped. Just like that the man's heart seemed to just give out. He fell to the side still tied the chair he was sitting on, his face set in a grin, blood red eyes staring, eternally amused.

'Shit, I think he's dead,' Bobby said.

'Mh hm,' The Pits said, after checking for a pulse.

'What do think it means, "The Ten Lords are Leaping?'

'Donno.'

'Come on man, help me out here, what am I gonna do? I need to bring back more than that.'

'Probably,' The Pits said. He had finished packing up his little case and was walking out the door.

'Thanks a lot, Pits,' Bobby said. Then instantly regretted his tone.

'What was that?' The Pits said, stopping but not looking back.

'Nothing, I said thanks.'

'I thought so. Happy Christmas'

And he was gone. Bobby knew he was fucked. The Good Old Boys would storm Hambry and take over. No problems. But he wouldn't be alive to see it. He had been told not to kill the Vassal until he found out what was going on. He failed and that was it for him. The Pits had nothing to worry about. He was a consultant, a tool, not his fault if Bobby told him to push the mark too far. Bobby wasn't sure the man could even be killed anyway.

He only had one option: he had to find out what the Vassal meant. He knew who the Ten Lords were; bosses of a sort in Hambry, he had been told that much. It stood for Tenement Lords, they apparently lived on the top floor of tenement buildings. Nobody seemed to know why, there was a certain mystery to what went on in Hambry. All anyone knew was that a lot of drugs came in there and then got sold around the country. It was how it had always been. The Vassals would bring the drugs in and mule them to whatever big city the Lords sent them to and they would sell them and go back to Hambry with the money. The bosses were planning on moving in on Christmas day, that gave him two days, counting the one that was already almost gone. He didn't have the time or the resources to abduct another Vassal. He would have to go to Hambry himself.

Although he'd heard it was a shit pit, the place was worse than Bobby had imagined. It was a dead town. He got off the train at midday the day after. It was Saturday so expected to see people milling around shopping, market stalls in the high street, kids running around screaming at their mothers, but there was none of that.

Most of the shops were either derelict or in poor states of repair. He counted four pawn shops and eight charity shops before he got to the end of the high street, the only recognisable places were a Boots and a Morrisons and even they had seen better days. Even the Christmas lights looked like they couldn't be bothered and the dead pine tree they had at the end of the street topped it off. He didn't dare stop any of the zombie-like denizens of the town to ask about the tenements, he didn't know who might be working for the Lords and who might not.

Side streets that were even more depressing than the High street came off at irregular spurs. The haphazard angles made it look like it had just been cobbled together years ago without any planning. It would be so easy for the Good Old Boys to come down here and take over the shipments, and the whole town if they wanted to. He wondered to himself why they had never done it before.

The docks seemed to be a good a place as any to start looking for Vassals. Then, he figured, he could follow them to the Lords and find out for himself what it all meant. Even if he had to blow some fools away before they told him. When he had been inducted into the gang he had been given a gun. The police didn't bother them, most were in the bosses' pockets anyway, so he carried his piece stuffed into his trackie bottoms at the back, ready in case he needed it. He didn't think he would. This place was a joke.

A ship was being unloaded when he got there. Boxes and boxes were being taken off onto the carved stone pier by hand and put on trolleys. These were then pulled and pushed away from the docks in all directions. Brazen, he thought, no wonder, though. He hadn't seen a police station on his travels, and he doubted any coppers made it out this far. He spotted the one he would follow almost straight away. An old woman pushing an ancient looking pram away from the pier. She was bent in half at the waist and had a pronounced hunch, which was covered by a light brown cardigan. Her hair was in a tight, pink rinsed perm and she was having a bit of trouble pushing the weight up the hill. He wasn't going to help, but he could take his time following her, without anyone noticing.

He went to a shop on the seafront—one of two that were open—and bought an ice cream. He didn't think twice about doing this: go to the seaside, buy an ice cream; even though it was the middle of winter. Then he sat on a bench, slowly eating it as he watched the old woman make her way to the top of the hill.

Bobby almost finished his cone by the time she disappeared around the corner. He casually got up and walked toward the two buildings that marked the beginning of the street she had entered. The ground levelled out at this point so it stood to reason that she would have made some progress, but when he got there he couldn't see her at all. Had she gone into one of the first houses? No, even that would have been unlikely, he hadn't been that slow nor she that fast. Then he caught a glimpse of a light brown cardigan vanishing around a corner at the other end of the street. A hundred yards or more away. Impossible, he thought, but jogged up the street in spite of his disbelief. Again when he got to the next corner, slightly out of breath, the woman was well ahead of him. She had reached a door and was pushing a doorbell by the side. He heard a quiet buzzing and saw her push the door open. He was easily two hundred yards from her now and would have to run full out to make it.

His foot just stopped the door closing when he got there thirty seconds later, gasping for breath now. How could she move so fast? He wondered. Maybe she wasn't the same woman. But he had seen the same stroller, the same cardigan, the same tightly curled pink rinsed hair.

Before he went in, he craned back to take a look. From the outside it looked like a row of Victorian houses. Four stories high and probably twenty houses along. Looking into the building it was clear that this one, at least, had been converted into flats. The hallway was dirty and dark. There were bags of rubbish with little clouds of flies above them outside the doors on either side of the corridor. The old woman was gone. No matter, he thought, he would find someone in this building who would tell him what the hell was going on here. Then he would go back home and tell the bosses what he had found. He'd surely get a promotion for this. It would be the best Christmas ever.

He wanted to be in and out fast, so he tried each door, left and right he jiggled handles to see if anyone forgot to lock up. The plan was to break in, put the gun to the occupant's head and make them tell him. It would be a cinch.

The corridor bifurcated at the end and Bobby followed the right limb. Then it happened again, and again. By now he was sure that the facade of the Victorian houses was just that. The buildings behind had been knocked together and the whole street was one long tenement. He tried to find his way back to the front door after trying his twentieth apartment and found it locked, but he couldn't find his way. Each fork he came to, he turned left where he had turned right and vice versa but he kept coming to dead ends. There were no windows, only door after door to be seen and every one with exactly the same shitty plastic wreath on the door, no numbers, no distinguishing marks.

Then he saw her, the old woman, she was rounding a corner. Bobby thought she must spend her life doing that. He sprinted to where she had been. Gone. But this time she'd come to a dead end. There was only one door on the right at the end of a short spur. There was nowhere else she could have gone. Bobby approached the door quietly and carefully tried the handle. It turned, stiffly but surely. He took his gun from his trousers and held it in front of him. He didn't want to get jumped by an old granny did he? The thought made him smile. Not the kind of smile that comes unbidden from amusement but rather the kind forced in a manner that hopefully promotes confidence. How had these people stayed on top for so long? He wondered. How were they so open about it all? So seemingly untouchable? Bobby pushed the thought from his head. They'll find out all about untouchable when the bosses come down on them.

Once the latch was released Bobby flung the door open, ready to put a bullet in that old bitch's head if she made a wrong move. But she was gone, vanished. The room was a bare cube; no en-suite, no walk in wardrobe, no windows, no other doors. A bald light bulb in the middle illuminated the bare concrete walls. Bobby walked around the circumference and found exactly nothing. There wasn't even a fireplace that she could have escaped through like old St. Nick. A real smile touched Bobby's lips at this, vanishing when he saw the thing in the centre of the room.

He had missed it at first because it was drawn onto the ground. It was a perfect circle inscribed with chalk with a five-sided star drawn inside, each point touching the circle. From where Bobby was, it looked the right way up, but from the door it would have been upside down. A fact which disquieted him for reasons unknown. He wanted to get rid of his unease and felt that if he stood on top of the shape it would seem less…wrong. In fact, he was compelled to stand on it, his feet made their way to the exact centre all by themselves. Bobby had no choice but to comply.

He stood facing the door, so the star would be the right way up. That wasn't right. There was a pressure in his head that said he must turn around. His feet, again, complied. Bobby looked down at them in disbelief. How could they betray him like that, his own feet. Suddenly the cold in the room was replaced with a furnace-like heat. It was coming from in front of him. He knew he mustn't look up from his feet, the pressure in his head said so.

'What the fuck?' Bobby said, as he did exactly as he had just told himself not to do and looked up.

The thing didn't answer. Bobby wasn't sure if it could, as—assuming it wasn't an ultra-realistic mask—it had the head of a boar. This slobbering grunting boar's head, replete with massive tusks, was perched atop a heavily muscled torso and what looked like the back legs of a giant goat. Bobby fell to his knees in front of this seven-foot beast. The pressure increased and burst sending streams of blood from his nose. The beast licked its massive chops, saliva frothing and dripping from its snarling lips. Bobby saw the monster's massive phallus, hardening as it bared down on him just before he blacked out.

Bobby awoke cold and utterly unable to move. At first he thought he was dead or paralysed. Then managed to lift his right shoulder slightly and realised that his wrist was tied down. Similar experiments revealed that both arms and legs and his head were in the same situation. He was lying on a cold hard surface like stone or something.

As his brain finally accepted his predicament, Bobby became aware of movement in his periphery. By wriggling his head slightly, he found that he could look a little more to his right than his left so he could almost see what it was. Robed and hooded figures were dancing around where he lay. Their robes were open in the front and he could see that they were naked underneath. Despite everything he blushed. But the sight of them being naked brought new realisation to his own body. The cold, it was because he was utterly naked too. Indignation pushed everything else aside. How dare they do this to one of the Good Old Boys. Didn't they know who they were messing with? He tried to say this but realised that he couldn't. His mouth was stuffed with something. At best he could make some annoyed sounds in his throat, but when he tried too hard he gagged.

The dancing got faster and faster, the people spinning and writhing in a terrifying primal dance. Bobby thought he would go mad. Then they stopped. It was sudden and somehow worse than the dancing. The dancers parted and into the circle came the old woman with the brown cardigan still pushing her pram. Her arthritic shuffling made him wonder again how she kept escaping him. Then as suddenly as the dancers had stopped, the old woman leaped onto the table standing astride him. She was uglier than he thought. She didn't just look old, her face looked inhuman. It was sunken and shrivelled like an ancient hag's but she had teeth, row upon row of little needles in her grinning mouth. Her eyes were almost all black only a tiny sliver of white showed at the sides. She shrugged off her clothes like she was shedding a skin and revealed an emaciated twisted body that was more animal than human, with skinny lupine legs ending in patent leather shoes and a row of three empty hanging dugs on each side of her torso.

She shrieked, arms raised in a victory v, claws protruding from her stubby fingers. Bobby's bladder released at the sight of those claws and vicious looking teeth. Spittle boiled from her mouth as she screamed in delight, drops of it landed on Bobby's exposed skin and burned like acid. She crouched down and sniffed at Bobby's urine and let out a ferocious cackle. Then she tore the gag from his mouth and relieved herself into his screaming mouth, hot burning liquid pouring out over his mouth and eyes. He gagged and spat, but the flow was relentless. When she finally finished she drew back her clawed hand and readied herself for a blow across Bobby's face.

'Enough!' an explosive voice exclaimed.

The beast stopped as if frozen. The only part that moved was its ears. Then it twitched its clawed hand again.

'I said: enough,' the voice bellowed.

The thing on top of Bobby sprang from him and flitted away like an animal stung by a fire.

'Why do you defile our place of worship?' the voice asked.

Bobby wasn't sure if it meant him or not, but he sobbed apologies and promises none the less as tears ran from his eyes.

'Never mind your apologies. Answer my question.'

The intrinsic authority in the voice brought Bobby back to his senses.

'I…I came to find out about the Lords,' Bobby said. 'The Ten Lords, I heard they were Leaping.'

Unkind laughter erupted all around Bobby. Both dancers and the voice were laughing at him. Mocking him.

'What?' Bobby said, suddenly indignant. 'Listen, you don't know who you're dealing with. You freaks better tell me what's going on with the Lords or the bosses will come down on you hard.'

The laughter stopped abruptly.

'You would not understand. There are no words for it in any of the modern tongues,' the voice said, quieter now. More dangerous. 'But I will say this: once we have Leaped, we will have need to fear nothing. From anyone ever again.'

'If you have nothing to fear then why am I tied here? Why don't you let me go? I can tell the bosses not to bother,' Bobby said.

He didn't really believe them. Nothing could stand in the way of the Good Old Boys. They would take this little turd of a town, easy. But he had to get back to report. To tell them to be careful. To tell them that these people were crazy. He decided he would say nothing about the monsters when he got back, who would believe him? All he had to do to get away was convince these freaks that he was afraid. Bobby had a gift for lying. He would be out of this in no time.

'But you can't go,' the voice said in answer to his question. 'We have a ceremony to perform and you are an important part. And besides, you defiled our home, for that you must pay.'

Bobby opened his mouth to say something else but the gag was shoved back in and he started to tilt. The table he was on was now at forty-five degrees. In front of him was a mirror that he had missed that last time. It allowed him to see himself. He was on a kind of altar surrounded by candles, which were in turn surrounded by the people in the robes. The owner of the voice was nowhere to be seen, but he started speaking again. This time Bobby didn't understand what he was saying, or chanting more like. It was repeating phrases in a language Bobby had never heard.

As soon as it started chanting the robed ones started dancing again. As the words got faster, so too did the dancing. They shed their robes and were now dancing naked, old and young, men and women, they looked like ordinary people, but their eyes were glazed. Like they had taken some of the stuff from the docks.

Now they were a blur twisting and writhing around in a tight circle. Then Bobby noticed movement from above. The shape he had seen before, the upside down star inside a circle. This time it was on the roof and there was a slit in the middle, a ragged puffy slit out of which a cloven hoof came. Followed by another. Bobby knew what was coming out of the symbol, what it was giving birth to.

The chanting increased in volume and speed now, the people nothing more than a fleshy ring spinning around him. A muscular male torso was coming from the slit in the ceiling now; except he didn't think it was in the ceiling at all, it looked more like an orifice of some goddess. His head rang with the noise and the movement. The bindings around him were tight as ever then the thing in the ceiling completed its emergence and landed on the floor, soundlessly. Everything ceased.

Bobby was looking into the black piggy eyes of the boar's head, its snarling snout frothing and dripping. The circle of people around him closed in tighter. They had knives in their hands now, long thin blades atop shiny metal hilts. Three steps and they were on him, the knives all converging at his solar plexus.

At a squeal from the boar's head they pierced him. Thirteen sharp points puncturing his skin deeply. He tried to cry out but choked on his gag. The blades drew out from the centre in a starburst pattern. He could both see it in the mirror and feel the steel scraping over ribs and sternum, pulling and snagging on the soft skin of his stomach.

All of them took a step back at once and Bobby saw the shape more clearly in the mirror. The table was at such an angle that his blood ran into channels in the surface and collected in a bowl at the foot of the table. The boar's head squealed in delight and chomped its jaws at the sight of the blood. Bobby started to feel lightheaded.

The beast approached him. It took the bowl, now mostly full, in both hands and raised up. Bobby's blood poured into the open jaws and onto the muscular chest. Its squeals became a growl as the bowl emptied, the beast throwing it on the floor. It approached bobby with unnatural speed and sniffed at his chest, saliva dripping onto his open wounds.

The second last thing Bobby saw before he died was the reflection of a massive head darting forward and pulling back with ferocious speed.

The last thing he saw was the mouthful of intestine it chomped through right in front of his face. In that moment he pitied whoever the bosses sent down to Hambry. Once the rest of the Lords Leaped, if they hadn't already, there would be no hope. No trace of anyone they sent would ever be found.

Nine Ladies Dancing - Daryl Lewis Duncan

I KILLED THE ENGINE, popped the keys in my coat pocket and pulled out the little slip of paper I had taken from the newsagent's window. "Housesitter required: Christmas Eve to Boxing Day. Owner away on business and has pets that need looking after. Good rate of pay. Call the number below."

"So, honey, this is the place then?" I said as I tried my best to pat down her curly head. It was an impossible task. She pulled away, smiling. "It's huge."

She was right. I didn't realise it was going to be such a fine looking house. It could hold about two flats the size of ours. I checked my watch. We were a little late but I'm sure they would understand with the weather. "Come on, honey, let's get out of the cold. We can get our things later." She didn't take much persuasion and was at the front door before me. It opened slowly and a face appeared from the darkness of the hall. It was a man, a really tall man with combed over hair and a pleasant face. "Hello, come in out of that cold."

I poked Emma on the arm because she had begun stamping the snow off her boots in the man's gorgeous wooden hallway floor. "Hey?" she said. The man laughed softly.

"You carry on, my dear. It can always be mopped up. Isn't the weather just terrible? I really am dreading the drive to the city."

He walked along the hall and turned into a large living room on the left. Emma was on his tail and turned just once to stick her tongue out. I heard a dog growl from the room.

"Now, old man, where's your manners."

The warmth from the fireplace hit me hard as I entered the room. It was beautiful. Two high backed arm chairs sat on either side of the roaring fire. There was a huge corner type settee in the middle of the room and bookcases all the way along the back wall. I thought about our own shitty living room. There wasn't enough room to swing a cat.

"Let me take your coats. Please, make yourself at home and don't mind Ralph. He's a bit wary of strangers but once he sees that you mean no harm he will probably go back to sleep. You can pet him if you like, Emma. Behind the ears is his favourite."

He took our coats and left the room. I could hear footsteps from a room above. I had assumed he lived alone. Perhaps it was another dog. I really wasn't a pet person but if this guy stuck by the payment he had mentioned on the phone then I would make myself a pet person for the weekend.

"Isn't he gorgeous, mum?" Emma said. The big hound was on his back now, all four legs sticking up and enjoying a good old belly rub. I made a note for Emma to wash her hands before we had supper.

"I'm so sorry," the man said as he came back into the room, hand extended for a shake, "My name's James. I'm so caught up in preparing for the trip, I've forgotten my manners."

His hand was warm and the handshake firm. "I'm Jenny and this is Emma. Emma, say hello to James." She got up and shook his hand too.

"Do you mind me asking why you have to go the city for Christmas? I asked. I hoped he didn't mind me too nosey. He smiled, drew a cigarette from his pocket, lit it up and spoke.

"My wife's sister has passed away quite suddenly. We are attending her funeral on Boxing Day. I know, quite bad timing but these things happen. I just couldn't leave the house unattended for three days. I hope we aren't putting you out. It is Christmas after all?"

"No, not at all. Actually, it's a blessing to get out of our place for a few days. It's not the greatest place in the world, especially at this time of year. No, Emma and I have a few things planned. So, thank you for letting us stay." He blew the smoke away from me and smiled. A figure at the door caught my eye.

"Ahh, Diane, come meet Jenny and Emma." She didn't. She raised a hand in a quick gesture of hello. "We need to get going before the roads getting any worse."

That was it. Obviously not the social type or perhaps, we weren't really in her social circle. Emma stood up. "Goodbye , Diane." James's laughter filled the room. He rustled her hair and made his way out. "I have a list of stuff that needs doing. It isn't much. The cupboards are yours, the fridge is full and there is a small cellar of wine at the back of the kitchen. Make yourselves at home and we shall see you in a couple of days. Any questions?"

"Where's the other ones?" asked Emma. I gave her a dirty look.

"Oh, they will find you, my dear. Quite the independent sorts. Oh and one more thing. There may be a couple of gifts below the tree in the library. No peeking until tomorrow morning, mind. Take care ladies."

We walked him to the door. His wife sat stern-faced in the passenger seat and never once acknowledged us. They drove off and Emma waved until they the car was lost in the snowfall. I told Emma to wait in the living room while I unpacked the car. My fingers were numb by the time I brought in the last of the bags and closed the huge front door behind me.

We unpacked and put our own stuff where we could find a space. He wasn't joking when he said the fridge was packed. Emma helped and I put the kettle on while reading the list James had left on the big table in the middle of the kitchen. I helped Emma get up onto it. I read while she ate a bag of cheese and onion crisps. The big dog needed feeding twice a day and let out into the back garden whenever he stood at the door. There were two cats that needed feeding once a day, but just make sure their water dish was always full. That was it. This was going to be easy. I set the list back down on the table. "Should we go exploring, honey?" She jumped off the table and was out of the kitchen in a rush.

The house was amazing. Downstairs they had the living room, the kitchen, a small study and a huge library. Upstairs there were at least six bedrooms and a master bedroom that I didn't want to go into. It wouldn't be right. We decided to share the guest room at the opposite end of the corridor. It was massive with a four-poster bed, a dresser and an ensuite bathroom bigger than my own bedroom at home. I was actually looking forward to bedtime.

The big dog had moved to the hall when we came back downstairs. I ran to the kitchen and grabbed the box with our presents in it. Emma was already in the library. She stood by the tree.

"You okay, hun?" I asked setting the box down on the rug by the window. The tree was about twice the size of Emma. She stood gazing at it, lost in all the lights and bubbles.

"Mum, it's so beautiful. What are those?" she asked. She was pointing at the little silver foil covered people, hidden at various places around the branches. "They're chocolates. Do you want one?"

"Shouldn't I wait until tomorrow?" she asked, already taking one off the branch and opening it in an instant. She bit half and offered me the other. I took it. Oh, it was delicious.

"No, one's okay," I said, licking the chocolate from my front teeth.

We arranged each other's presents around the tree. It was pitiful really. One gift from Emma to myself and three from me to her. Sometimes I really hated the way things had turned out. I was just blessed to have a child that didn't really care for the material stuff. If she opened a parcel in the morning and found an orange she would hug the life from me in thanks.

12 Days Of Christmas 2016

"Mum?"

"What, sweetheart?" I asked as I stood up and kicked a cramp from my thigh. She was holding a beautifully wrapped box with her name on it. I took it from her. The paper looked expensive.

"There's one for you too. Should we open them? You always allow me to open one present before Christmas." Her face was a picture. I was tempted but I thought it rude.

"Let's just wait until morning. Are you tired?" I said knowing full well it would be hours before she was ready for bed. "No, not yet. Did you bring my drawing stuff? I want to make a drawing for James and his wife."

She spread out her paper and pencils all over the living room mat and I eased myself into one of the chairs with a glass of wine and a book. This was really living. If we had been back home right now, we would be huddled around the small electric heater trying to keep warm and dreading the many winter nights ahead. This was just Heaven.

I read a couple of chapters, sipped my wine, filled the glass and watched Emma as she created her masterpiece, on her belly, legs licking and relaxed. Perhaps someday we would be able to afford this kind of peace and luxury.

I could feel a tapping on my arm. Was I dreaming? My eyes pulled open and Emma stood in front of my chair with her finished piece.

12 Days Of Christmas 2016

"What you think?"

It was a wonderful picture of James, his wife and us two all standing beside a Christmas tree. She had even given Jame's wife a smiling face. I thought that a little generous.

"Oh, honey, it's wonderful. James will love it. What time is it?" I asked. She didn't answer and got back to her drawing. Perhaps it was the wine but I began to feel really tired. "Emma, I'm just going out for some fresh air, be back real soon."

"Mum?" she said as I got up. She was pointing at my cigarette packet on the arm of the chair. No fooling my girl.

The step was cool on my bum but at least the weather had eased a little. A huge moon stared down at me and cast a white glow over the huge yard. I was so taken by it that half my cigarette burned out without as much as drag. I lit another. The excitement of Christmas morning was building. I couldn't wait to see Emma's sweet face when she opened her present. I already knew what I was getting because I was with her when she bought it but that didn't matter. I would love it just the same. I watched as the smoke floated slowly from my mouth. For the first time in months, we were happy. Something touched my leg. It was one of the cats. He was a handsome chap, completely black. He purred and rubbed himself against me. I went to stroke his head. Emma screamed.

The cat ran off as I scrambled quickly to my feet and sprinted to the living room. Emma was crouched in front of the fire with her arms across her face. The poor girl was shaking. I rubbed her back and pulled her close. "What is it, honey?" Did you spook yourself?"

"Someone spoke my name."

I paused before answering. Looking around the room which was silly really.

"Listen, mum shouldn't have left you alone for so long. It's just a large house with many draughts and creaks. What say we get a good book and go up to that fabulous bed? It won't be long until morning," I said standing up and placing the guard over the fireplace. It was dying down but I didn't take any chances.

At the top of the stairs, I was about to turn off the landing lights when Emma stopped, looked at me and spoke, "It was a girl." I swallowed. Okay, that's a nice thought at this time of night. As Emma skipped past me, I actually did take a sneaky look down into the hallway.

Emma was in bed before I hadn't even reached the room. I got changed while she picked a book. It was one we had read over many times but that was okay.

Once we were both tucked up, I began to read. Emma mouthed along, keeping her eye on the lines, ready to turn the page.

I waited for her to turn the final page. She didn't. Looking over I saw her staring out into the landing. Her tiny hand gripped my wrist.

"Ouch, Emma, what's up?" I said. Her nails had actually dug into my skin.

"I thought I saw a face looking around the door. Do you think it's the girl again?"

This time the shivers crept right through my back. I decided then it was time we got some sleep. Emma's mind was doing overtime because of all the excitement.

"Okay, honey, let's try and get our heads down. I'll even keep the light on for a bit, okay?"

With that, she turned her back towards the door and rested her head on my arm. I took a quick look at the door, laughed gently to myself and closed my eyes.

Next morning, Emma was still asleep when I awoke. It was so lovely under that big heavy quilt. They certainly had a taste for comforts. I didn't want to leave but I wanted to grab a coffee and a cigarette while it was still early. I eased myself out from under the covers, popped on the same clothes as yesterday and made my way downstairs.

The big hound was standing at the front door. Damn, I had forgotten to let the poor boy out the night before.

"Apologies, big man. There you go. He plodded out the front door and sniffed around a little. I left him to it and went to the kitchen. I wondered what kind of fancy coffee they would have here. My taste buds buzzed on my tongue thinking about it.

I placed my cup beside me on the front step and watched the dog having a grand dump to himself over by a flowerbed. I smoked my cigarette. It was a bright morning with just a few flickers of snow now and again. Perfect for a Christmas day. "Mum,"

I stubbed my cigarette, pulled myself and ran towards the biggest hug of the year. "Happy Christmas sweetheart. Can I get you something before we open presents?" she shook her head. Her lip trembled a little. I thought she was going to cry. I felt my own eyes tear up too. This was special. This was really going to be the best Christmas ever.

"Okay, let's go to the library." Once the hound was back inside I closed the door. He fell in a heap. "Not a fan of Christmas then?"

12 Days Of Christmas 2016

There was wrapping paper strewn across the large mat in front of the tree. I reached around the back and switched on the lights. After a few seconds, the whole tree lit up in gold and silver, twinkling in the dull light of the library. "Well, honey, what you got there?"

She held up a wooden art set, one of those fold away types, one-half filled with paints, the other all pencils and crayons. Her face said it all. I got a grand hug for that one.

"Your turn," she said handing me a perfume bottle shaped present.

"Oh my, wonder what it could be?" I said, my eyes wide, mouth open. Emma laughed as I opened the paper carefully.

"Oh, my favourite smelly. Thank you, pumpkin, you really shouldn't have." She hugged me, called me silly and then it was her turn again.

The next gift she opened was an old teddy bear that I picked up for a few quid in a charity shop. I had spent a couple of days at the beginning of the month sewing him up and making him smart and handsome again. " I will call him, Arthur." Said Emma. Well, at least she had named him, that was a good sign. I opened my last gift, a bottle of wine, pretended to open it straight away and got the most serious look.

12 Days Of Christmas 2016

While she was talking to Arthur, I reached down and pulled her last present from under the tree. This was the one I was excited about. "Here you go, honey. I hope you like it."

Her little fingers darted across the paper, tearing it slowly, peeking a little as she went. She stopped when she realised what it was. I leaned back into the chair. I knew there was an almighty hug coming after this one.

She stood up and held the dress to her body. It looked a perfect length. "Do you like it?" A tear fell down her cheek. That done it for me. I couldn't hold back. Ever since the day we had seen that dress in all its red velvet glory in an expensive shop on Main Street, I knew exactly what she was getting for Christmas. It was expensive but Emma was good with her things. "Can I try it on now, Mum, please?" she asked. I nodded.

My what a picture. "My God, Emma, you look so gorgeous. How does it feel?" I asked, wiping the last remaining tear from my cheek.

"It's my favourite thing in the whole world. I love you, Mum," she said and didn't hug me. Blew a kiss instead and said she didn't want to wrinkle her dress. "So, how about some breakfast and then we can watch some of the old Christmas movies on TV?"

"What about the gifts from James and his wife?" I had forgotten about those. I assumed they wouldn't be much.

They were paying me plenty for being here for the weekend without going to too much expense. At least I hoped they didn't. Emma handed me a small box. I shook it. Nothing.

"What is it, mum? Can I see?" Emma asked on her tiptoes, peering over the box. Inside was the most beautiful ankle bracelet I had ever seen. It looked expensive. I didn't even recognise the name on the box. It wasn't from a shop in town, that's for sure.

"Help me put it on, honey." She did and I loved it. I was so busy admiring it that I hadn't seen Emma open her gift. She had her back to me. "Honey?"

She didn't hear me. "Emma?" I asked louder. She turned around with some strange device in her hands. It looked like a large cup or something similar.

"Mum, what is it?" she asked handing it to me. I took it, it was heavy. It was made of some kind of metal. Inside where nine different pictures of dancing girls. Emma stood beside me and placed a finger on the side of the thing. It spun slowly. She did it again, harder this time. The cylinder inside spun around. I looked in but it was just a blur. Emma knelt down and looked into the side of the thing where there were a few vertical openings. Her face lit up.

"Oh, mum, look," she said. I turned my head to the side, spun it once again and peered into one of the holes. It was wonderful, the nine girls all came together in a simple dance routine which looked more like a curtsy but still fun. What a curious gift.

"Do you like it, Emma?" I asked, hoping the antique nature of the thing hadn't disappointed her. "Emma?" I asked again. She was fixed on it and a wide beaming smile crossed her face. I guessed she was happy. I left her to it and went to make us both some breakfast.

The pan spat back at me a couple of times as I turned the bacon. While it simmered I buttered some bread and arranged them on both plates. "Emma, this is ready, honey," I said. She didn't reply. "EMMA?"

After turning the gas down low I went back to the library. Emma was still sitting where I had left her, spinning the dancers. I touched her shoulders and she jumped.

"Breakfast, sweetheart," I said. She stood up, bringing the thing with her. James had really nailed it with this gift. I could hear the whirr it made as she followed me to the kitchen.

Emma wolfed the cereal down in a few spoonfuls and grabbed two pieces of toast from the tray. "Can I take these, mum?" she asked. Okay, I guess this was going to be the way Christmas day panned out. As long as she was happy, I was happy. I washed up and decided to have a long shower.

Coming back downstairs I decided to see if they had any old Christmas albums around. I toweled my hair dry and entered the living room, fully expecting Emma to be there with her bits and pieces. She wasn't. I tried the library and the kitchen. "Emma?" She couldn't have gone outside without asking me first. She wasn't that type of girl. Something caught my eye in the garden. I was wrong.

The wind cut right through me as I walked to where she was. There, she was, walking in circles with the zoetrope in her hand, spinning it, lost in the pictures. "EMMA?" I said reaching for her shoulder. She actually jumped as if I had startled her. She was bound to have seen me approach. "Come inside, honey, it's freezing." She stared at me, hand poised on the wheel again. "It's where they used to dance."

"Who did?" I asked, biting my bottom lip against the shivers. She spun the wheel again and held it up for me to see.

Inside the nine figures spun around and performed the most simple of movements. To be honest it wasn't the most impressive thing in the world but Emma liked it and that's what matters. Emma spun it faster. To keep her happy, I kept watching. The figures sped up and became one. This lone dancer's hands reaching above them in fear and then falling. I pulled my face away. "Jesus."

"Did you see them, mum?" she asked walking past me towards the house. I didn't answer. I just jogged to catch up with her. I needed a coffee and perhaps some hot chocolate for Emma. The hound was sniffing around the back door as we approached. Emma patted his big head. He didn't look at me. Dumb dog.

The coffee was the cure. Emma sipped from her cup and stared at the Christmas tree. She was quiet. I didn't like it. "Do you want to play games or something?" I asked setting my cup down beside the chair.

"No, the time for games is over. You need to accept that and move on."

My mouth dropped open. I didn't know whether to laugh or what.

"Excuse me, Emma?" I said.

She turned, "Yeah, hide and seek? I love to hide and seek." Had she not realised what she had said?

"You go first, mum. I'll count."

I tried not to make it too hard for her. We didn't really know our way around the house yet. I stood behind the big heavy curtain at the front door and waited. The old velvet smelled of damp and tickled my nose a little too much. She counted slowly to twenty. I tried not to sneeze. "Ready or not."

That was it. No, here I come. I waited. Emma was usually good at this, but then our place wasn't as big and hiding places were few and far between.

I peeked out between the gap in the curtain and the door. The hallway was empty. Where had she gone looking? A few more minutes and I'd give up.

I could hear her talking to someone. "Emma?" I said, untangling myself from the curtains.

She had never left the kitchen and remained in the exact same spot, hands still covering her eyes but long finished counting.

"I'm here with my mum, you don't need to be afraid anymore. We will help you? I like the way you dance. Can you teach me?"

I shook her. No response. I forced her hands from her eyes. "Emma, what is wrong with you? Who are you talking too?"

"The dancers." The zoetrope was on the floor beside her, spinning around, making that horrible whirring sound. My foot connected with it and sent it across the tiles, broken. Emma screamed. I slapped her on the face. Not hard, but hard enough for her to stop, look straight up at me and smile. "You shouldn't have done that, mum."

"Emma, you need to stop this stuff, we were playing a game. You didn't come. Perhaps James shouldn't have got you that thing. When we get back home, I'll take you to the toy shop uptown. Okay?" She nodded.

"Okay, my turn," she said running from the room. Okay, that went surprisingly well. I covered my eyes, counted slowly and gave her time to find a good hiding place. I owed her that at least.

"Okay, I'm coming to get you, ready or not."

I had heard her footsteps on the stairs so I knew she wasn't downstairs, but I had a look around anyway all the time talking loudly. I could picture her up there somewhere, giggling away, thinking she had me fooled.

"Okay, I'm coming upstairs now, going to find you real soon." A giggle from under the stairs. Okay. She was better at this than I thought. I tiptoed back down the stairs, along the hall and opened the door under stairs. Nothing.

Footsteps on the landing. I've got you now. I ran up the stairs, half expecting to see her dart into one of the bedrooms. I wasn't quick enough. The landing was empty.

"Emma, I know you're up here," I said, hoping for a giggle. The kitchen door slammed shut. Okay, deep breath, that was obviously just the hound or the wind. I continued along the landing. All the bedroom doors were closed tight. I listened at the first couple. Silence.

I was about to lean into the next one for a listen and the door handle moved back into position. Ha, there you go, Emma. I knocked it gently. "Ready or not?" A voice from downstairs, "Mum?"

I pulled my hand away from the door handle right away. I walked backward from the door, turned and looked over the railing to the hallway below. Emma was standing there with her hands reaching up to me. Her face was pale, mouthing words I couldn't hear. I took off down the stairs, almost tripping over my feet near the bottom.

"Come here, honey, what's wrong?" I asked. The girl turned. It wasn't Emma. My hands hung in mid-air, the girl laughed and ran away along the hall.

"Mum, help me," Emma screamed from upstairs. I turned quickly and made for the stairs again. Something gripped my ankle. A girl about Emma's age was holding it tight and trying to rip off my bracelet. Her nails were deep into my skin. I cried out. "Let, fucking, go,"

She moved away, crawling backward across the hallway. I touched my bracelet and my fingers came away sticky with blood, my own. I moved slowly up the stairs. Where the hell did these girls come from? Where they from a house nearby? Why didn't they speak? I had so many questions. A scream from the bathroom dragged me from my thoughts.

My foot kicked hard against the bathroom door and it swung all the way in and rattled hard against the edge of the bath. The room was empty. I slumped to the floor, back resting against the heavy wooden door. I mouthed Emma's name but hadn't the energy to utter any voice. I closed my eyes. Waves of tiredness swept over me, my legs felt heavy and the cuts around my bracelet stung. Beyond the noise of my own thoughts, I could hear music. It was Christmas music, one of those old songs from a black and white movie. I picked myself up, stumbled from the bathroom and took my time going down the stairs. Children's laughter echoed from the library. Emma's own sweet laugh was one of them. I felt like storming in there and giving them all a piece of my mind. Their joke had gone too far. I would get their parents numbers and call them. I mean, why were they not at home on Christmas day, it just wasn't right.

The library was empty. The needle skipped at the end of the record. The song was over. Lifting the needle gently and placing it back in its holder, I closed the lid of the stereo and there were three sharp knocks on the library door. I swung around. Laughter again. More than one voice and bare feet running along the wooden hall. "Fuck this," I screamed and ran out into the hall. I slipped on the polished surface and went crashing into coat stand, knocking it over. Most of the coats had landed on top of me. I began pushing them away. I couldn't. Something or someone was holding them down. More laughter. "Get the fuck off of me."

I kicked out, wrestled with the coats but still couldn't break free. It felt like they were all piled on top of the coats, pressing down onto me. I started to panic, breath catching in my throat. "Emma? Emma, please honey, make them stop," I called out. They did. The weight seemed to ease off a little. I felt a small hand reach under the heaviest of coats and touch my own. I gripped it. It was cold and clammy. With my other hand, I pushed the last of garments away from me. A small girl's face appeared inches from my own, thin lips forming a gentle smile and without warning let out a piercing scream.

I don't know how long I lay under the coats afraid of seeing that hideous face again. What had they done to my Emma? What kind of mother was I, lying here when I should be finding her and taking her away from this place? The thoughts of what people would say gave me a new heart to pull myself together and sort this out. I wouldn't let those little bitches ruin my daughter's Christmas. We still had boxing day to look forward to. I rose up and kicked the coats out of my way. There were some leaves in the hall. The front door lying wide open. Okay, so they had left or at least had gone outside. I thought about putting some shoes on but imagined the cool snow would keep me alert. I called out for Emma as I reached the door. It slammed shut. I grabbed the handle. It wouldn't turn. I punched and kicked the door until my toes and knuckles bled. Tears tasted salty on my lips. I was shaking.

"Mum?"

Emma stood about ten yards up the hall. Her dress was filthy.

"Emma, honey. Come to mum, would you?" She stayed in the same spot. Her face expressionless. "Emma, please?"

She lifted her hands to her throat and began to throttle herself. I screamed and ran to her. She walked backward in the opposite direction. She began choking, face growing paler. "Emma, stop that now," I said reaching for her. Many hands held me back. Small bare arms around my waist, hands pulling at my clothes, more arms around my legs and the voices, eight girls all whispering my name, as I screamed for them to let me go. My baby was dying right before my eyes.

Emma was right in front of me now. She had stopped strangling herself but I could see the marks where hands had been. "You broke it, mum. They were happy in there. They were dancing."

The hands all fell away from me and the girls, eight of them all walked around me to join Emma. They were all dressed in nightgowns. They all had the same marks on their necks as Emma. From behind her back, Emma brought the broken zoetrope. It was in three pieces and irreparable.

"I didn't mean to, you were just acting so strange. Who are these girls? Hello?"

They had vanished. I stood alone, my heart racing, my body sore. I let my feet carry me to the library. I had no real reason to go there or anywhere.

I stood at the window. Most of the snow had melted away. All that was left was a few patches here and there. Something was moving at the far end of the garden. I cupped my hands and pressed my nose against the glass. It was hard to see but in the glow of the large garden lamps, I saw them. All nine girls dancing in a circle. They looked happy. I watched them dance for as long as I can remember until a harsh light exploded through the window.

I heard voices in the hallway. "I've found her. Officers, in here, please." Heavy boots on the wooden hall. A female voice. "Jenny, love? A hand on my shoulder. I turned.

The woman smiled at me. She looked familiar. "It's okay, we're going to take you back now. You had us worried." They led me from the library, up the hall.

"Darren, remind me when we get back to get that tracking bracelet looked at. It must be faulty," the woman said to her male friend. Something caught my eye. Something I hadn't seen before. On the wall, there was a large oil painting of James and Diane. It had been ripped across the middle. To the side of the painting in large graffiti paint was the word, 'MURDERERS'.

The man noticed it too. "Miss, wasn't this a Foster Home or something a few years back?" he asked the woman.

"Yes, it was but it was closed down after what happened. Come on, Jenny, let's get you back to the hospital."

12 Days Of Christmas 2016

Eight Maids Milking - C.L. Raven

EVERYONE CRAVES THE PERFECT Christmas.

No-one's prepared to make sacrifices for it.

Angel weaved through drunken guests sporting terrible Christmas jumpers, reindeer headbands or Santa and elf hats. Christmas songs played on repeat, like every year. She smiled as her sister, Holly, lured her victim under the mistletoe with nothing more than a flirtatious smile and unspoken promises of pleasure. Throughout the room, her other sisters, Ivy, Carol, Donna, Seren, Belle and Eve trapped men under mistletoe, bunches of it hanging like corpses from a gallows. All the sisters were dressed as sexy Santas with glittery red lipstick and eye shadow. Though the lucky men would never get to enjoy the presents inside their stockings.

Angel swiped a slice of Christmas cake off a passing waitress's tray and basked under the last sprig of mistletoe, watching her prey as she bit the head off a marzipan elf.

Someone grabbed her around the waist, grinding his body against hers. "Hey sexy Claus, fancy sitting on my lap and tugging my cracker?"

She elbowed the groper in the stomach and spun free, keeping hold of her cake. His party hat slipped over one eye and he'd drunk more sherry than St Nick on Christmas Eve. His hideous jumper boasted a snowman with a carrot penis and 'Christmas came early' written in suspicious looking snow. Her sisters ensnared decadent delights with their mistletoe. Hers sent out siren songs to the human equivalent of slushy January snow that refused to melt and made your boots soggy.

It was enough to turn anyone into a grinch.

"You can't refuse a kiss under the mistletoe." He broke off a sprig and looped it over his belt. "I'll let you lick my candy cane."

"No thanks. Small parts are a choking hazard."

A man looking embarrassed in his elf costume tapped Pervy Claus on the shoulder. "Leave her alone."

"She's asking for it, dressing like that," he muttered as he staggered away.

"You're asking to have your chestnuts roasted on an open fire, but I've restrained myself," Angel retorted, lobbing the decapitated elf at him.

The elf smiled shyly. "You look stunning."

"Thank you." Angel grabbed his dangling bells and pulled him close for a kiss. "Merry Christmas." As his knees buckled, she smiled and whispered in his ear, "a kiss may ruin a human life."

Angel finished tying her prey's feet with tinsel. More tinsel bound his hands, while coloured fairy lights wound around his body.

"This is…interesting bondage," he said as she straddled him.

"I'm feeling festive."

She'd heard her sisters entering the shed but she rarely found a good gift so wanted to savour hers. Many people played with an early Christmas present on Christmas Eve. She refrained from kissing him on the lips until she'd won the prize from his Christmas cracker – her Silent Night lipstick would ruin the romantic moment.

After he'd surrendered to the sleeping dust, she slipped a butcher's hook around the tinsel tying his feet and pulled him off the bed. She dragged him outside to the shed, leaving a trench in the snow. Icicle lights framed the windows, the roof wore a snowy shroud and a wreath decorated the door. Reindeer roamed free and smoke danced from the chimney. It resembled grottos seen in snow globes and expensive shopping centres.

Pushing open the door, she saw the other presents hanging from hooks like stockings above a fireplace. The maids had attended several parties world-wide this evening, and never returned empty-handed. Angel attached the hook to a chain then pulled until her toy dangled upside down.

"Capturing them is too easy. It almost ruins the fun. Can't we take the reindeer and sleigh and hunt them? Like how Father first collected elves."

"They must be willing," Belle pointed out. "Sexy Santas and mistletoe make men very willing."

As the clock struck midnight, welcoming in Christmas Eve, the sisters slid sharpened candy canes from their stockings and slit their prey's throats. Blood trickled down the men's faces and dripped into troughs which led into two Christmas pudding receptacles. The maids ran their hands down their gifts' limbs and torsos, squeezing to encourage the blood flow.

"This reminds me of milking cows," Holly said. "It'd be quicker with a milking machine."

"They don't have udders," Seren said.

Holly smirked and raised one eyebrow. "Don't they?"

Part of Angel wished she had kissed the groper. Nothing would give her greater pleasure than seeing him strung up, thrashing uselessly as the life drained from his body. But torture tended to spoil festivities.

"These are empty," Eve called, checking the men furthest into the shed.

Angel, Seren and Ivy helped Eve carry them to the workshop tables. A train track circled the room, like stitches on Frankenstein's monster. A wooden train shuddered beside the table.

"I love unwrapping presents." Angel sliced through the man's torso with her candy cane.

"Shopping for presents is my favourite part." Ivy's fingers skimmed down a man's arm. "There's so much eye candy. A girl could get greedy."

"Decorating the tree's the best part," Eve said.

Angel peeled back the man's skin and carefully removed his bones. An elf appeared beside her, scowling while she loaded his arms with the bones. Whilst the elves sported the stereotypical green outfits and short stature, they were far uglier than the happy green elves that infested Christmas stories. As though someone tried to carve facial features into raisins then gave them needle fangs and red eyes. More Nightmare Before Christmas than Babes in Toyland.

Angel would happily sacrifice them for a perfect Christmas but Father was enraged when she'd knocked an elf into the mincer. Spending the Christmas period being Santa's little helper in shopping centre grottos taught her killing elves wasn't worth the punishment. And the mince pies tasted bitter. Lusty teens kept trying to grab her baubles. Apparently, hanging the bad humbugs with festive ribbons and carving flaps into them like human advent calendars wasn't showing goodwill to all men.

She cleaned the skin, tanned it then spread it on the table. "Most of this is useable."

Donna and Carol cut the skin into the required pattern then stitched pieces together.

"Why are some so hairy?" Donna snatched up a razor and shaved her back piece. "It makes work for us."

"Why not put an ad in the paper?" Angel asked. "'Willing sacrifices needed for the perfect Christmas. Only hairless men need apply'."

"I'm tempted, but the mortal realm has 'laws'. Advertising for willing victims is probably illegal."

Belle separated the organs into 'edible' and 'offal'. She laid the intestines to one side and fed the inedible organs into the furnace. The flames devoured the offerings, sending smoke into the sky and filling the grotto with the stench of burning meat, like a kitchen on Christmas day. She placed the edible organs into a train carriage then sent it into the kitchen where Mother made mince pies from the meat. Mother's Secret Santa Pies were hugely popular. Every year people tried guessing the secret ingredient that made the pies so tasty. No-one ever guessed correctly. They all thought it was a special spice.

Angel sauntered around her gift. "Don, save me this back piece. I need new artwork for my bedroom wall." She pointed to the graveyard tattoo on her victim's back.

"You could buy artwork."

"I want to remember this night."

Angel pulled up a rocking horse and sat to watch the blood drain into the trough. The sparkling lights reflecting in the blood gave her that warm Christmassy glow. This time of year was enchanting.

Once there was enough blood, she decanted some into a large bauble, fetched a brush and got to work. She dipped her brush into the blood and painted red stripes onto stark white candy canes. Children loved these sweet treats so they had to be perfect. She propped them up until they dried and continued with the next batch. An elf gathered the dry ones to wrap in clear packaging which reminded her of transparent body bags. Seren joined her, singing along to the Christmas songs Father insisted were played. The elves hated the songs. They despised everything about Christmas and were miserable for the entire holiday season until they got drunk Christmas night. Then they were grouchy the following morning.

They finished the candy canes then Angel checked on the sleigh. The first sack of presents was already waiting to be loaded. Elves sawed, hammered and glued the sleigh together. Angel had been doubtful that human bones were a good building material for flying transport but the elves worked their magic every year and there hadn't been a single accident. Apart from the Christmas of '97 but the tribunal had cleared Father of drunk driving. And the pedestrian received a hefty compensation and extra presents to apologise for her amputated leg.

"New design?" Angel circled the sleigh.

"Father wanted it more aerodynamic," an elf grunted. "Pressure is on him to reduce delivery times due to the annual increase in children. Nearly 400,000 babies are born every. Fucking. Day. He's struggling to deliver to everyone in one night. I suggested a helpful gift of contagious diseases but apparently poisoning children isn't in the 'Christmas spirit'."

"So we slip condoms into the stockings for everyone of childbearing age," another elf added, gesturing to the condom boxes.

Someone had stacked them in the shape of Christmas trees. Angel picked up a box. Gingerbread flavour. She scanned the other flavours: Christmas pudding, Christmas spice, turkey, eggnog, candy cane, fruitcake, mince pie, mulled wine, Brussel sprouts. She dreaded to think what Snowman's Surprise tasted like.

"The stress of delivery is taking its toll on his heart," the second elf continued. "If people keep having kids, Father might die."

"Christmas is for children. Without them, there's no Father Christmas. Their belief keeps him alive."

"When he started this role, disease, poverty and violence meant a high infant mortality rate. Yes people were mass procreating due to lack of contraceptives and entertainment, but they rarely lived long. It was easier to deliver. Easier to prepare for too. It was more relaxed, not this manic pace we endure now. And the children were grateful for anything as long as it wasn't coal and a spanking from Krampus. Children today aren't happy if their present can't be plugged in and shown off. And the length of their lists! That sack is for one child. Nowadays the government give people money just to have kids. So they're breeding like rampant rabbits, not considering the consequences. And they're all living! Sucking the life out of Father with every selfish breath."

"It's like Christmas with the Kranks in here. Why not hire another Father Christmas?" Angel suggested. "Half his workload."

The second elf glared at her. "There can be only one."

12 Days Of Christmas 2016

Angel returned to her sisters. The elves were as joyful as finding a tooth instead of a coin in your Christmas pudding. She guessed their vendetta against children stemmed from working in the grottos. She'd only done it once and developed a murderous streak she never knew existed. They were there every year. No wonder their faces permanently resembled curdled eggnog.

Donna and Carol attached their finished handiwork to a rack and lowered it into the pudding of blood to soak. Ivy painted more skin black then allowed it to dry before stitching it together. Donna and Carol raised the rack. Blood dripped into the pudding like scarlet rain. In a few hours it would dry then Father would be able to wear his new leather suit. Ivy finished the stitching detailing on his boots and gloves then set them aside.

Father insisted on a new suit and boots every year. Delivering millions of presents through chimneys was hard, hot work. The leather protected him from cuts and scrapes from the bricks but it meant he sweated profusely. He refused to take his suit to the dry cleaners in case they asked awkward questions. Nowhere in children's picture books did it mention Father Christmas wearing a suit made from human skin and he wanted to keep it a mystery. Secrets were what made Christmas special.

Belle and Eve stuffed the sleigh seat cushion with hair taken from their gifts then used the remaining skin to cover the seat in a patchwork style and painted it black.

Once the bone sleigh had set, the elves busied themselves painting it with the remaining blood then coating it with a lacquer of tears. Human tears were harder to milk than blood. The maids tended to collect them at certain points of the year: Christmas, New Year's Eve and Valentine's Day. And when they were really desperate, celebrities' funerals were a great source. Due to the difficulty in obtaining tears, they'd experimented with different types of lacquer but nothing could beat the shine borne from suffering.

Angel found her sisters decorating the tree. Seren sprinkled glitter over eyeballs before hanging them from the branches. Holly and Ivy made a garland of festive fingers, each one with a different Christmas themed fingernail. Belle and Eve used glitter spray on the intestines before weaving them around the branches like sparkling snakes. Donna and Carol were making the most important decoration: the star for the top. Strictly speaking, it wasn't a star.

"It's your turn to do the honours." Donna offered the human head to Angel.

Grinning, Angel bounded up the stepladder and carefully positioned the head on top of the tree. It belonged to the man she'd kissed under the mistletoe. This made it even more special for her. His eyes hung from the branches.

12 Days Of Christmas 2016

"Light it up!" Angel called, attaching the wire.

Eve plugged it in. Fairy lights twinkled in the head's eye sockets. The maids cheered. As always, they had the most beautiful tree. The elves cut tree shapes from cereal boxes, painted them green and glued a tealight to each one. Sometimes they poked fairy lights through them in the shape of letters then arranged the trees to spell out rude words. Their sour spirit always failed to ruin the magic, however hard they tried.

"Is my suit ready?"

Father's rasping voice was quiet yet slipped into everyone's ears, whispering seductively into their minds.

"Put it on and we'll add the finishing touches," Donna said.

The sisters returned to the grotto where the suit hung. Tinkling bells approached the room. The sound of bells accompanied Father wherever he went. That's how children knew he was on their roofs, in their houses.

A black gnarled hand pushed the door open. The bells grew louder. Father stepped into the room, his scarlet eyes glowing brighter when he spied the suit.

"Every year you excel yourselves, sweet sisters," he rasped.

They beamed. He crept over to the suit. Without the bells, you would never know he was around. Father didn't look how the picture books depicted. Not yet. At seven feet tall, he made the elves look like children's toys. His body was the colour of coal, his long spindly arms and legs more suited to Halloween than Christmas. His crooked fingers and toes resembled spider legs, enabling him to scuttle swiftly and silently when he wasn't wearing his boots. His body was lean and rough, the same texture as aged tree bark.

"Your sacrifices grow stronger each year. The children will have the perfect Christmas their parents yearn for." He smiled, revealing silver needle teeth. The sisters smiled back, showing matching teeth. "Each year they long for the Christmas they see in books, on TV. Yet you are the only ones willing to sacrifice human souls to ensure it happens."

"People have been making human sacrifices to their gods since religion began," Eve said. "They worship you at this time of year. But they forget that success is built on blood."

He cupped her chin with his hand, his long fingers stroking her cheek. "You're right, my child."

Ivy and Seren took the suit down from the rack and helped him into it. Holly laced his boots. Carol fetched his new leather gloves. Angel grabbed scissors and entered the small room off the grotto. She switched on the lights. Rows of human heads greeted her. All were old men with bushy white beards. After they removed the heads, the sisters took time to wash and shampoo the beards until they were soft and fluffy. She carefully peeled all the beards off except from one then returned to the grotto, carrying the bearded head.

Belle fetched glue then the sisters stuck the beards to Father's suit cuffs. Donna fastened his belt then she and Angel removed the face from the bearded head. Father knelt and they laid it over his face. Eve placed his red hat on his head with a beard bobble and trim.

He murmured festive song lyrics from a forgotten language then rose. His body transformed, shrinking in height and ballooning outwards. His gnarled fingers became plump digits in his gloves. The face moulded to his own, the eyes opening to reveal soft brown human eyes. He smiled, displaying human teeth.

"How do I look?" His booming jolly voice echoed around the room.

"You look just like Father Christmas." Holly smiled.

"Ho! Ho! Ho!"

They clapped. Children believed Father Christmas was magical but they had no idea how magical he truly was.

After Father Christmas's departure, the sisters returned to their magnificent tree. They piled gifts for each other beneath its branches, every present neatly wrapped in leftover skin. The eyeballs on the tree swivelled, watching them. The fingers on the garland twitched, reaching for them. The head on top of the tree blinked, the lights inside its skull briefly dimming. Angel scampered up the ladder and placed a kiss on the head's lips.

"I know we've only just met but I'm excited we can spend Christmas together."

That was the best part about living in Father's magical land: no-one ever died at Christmas.

12 Days Of Christmas 2016

Seven Swans Swimming - Matthew Cash

WE WERE ALL EXCITED that day and the weather was perfect for it. The sun was blazing down from a blemish free sky, it had snowed again overnight and the crispness of the temperature meant it would most likely stay for a while. If it lasted for more than twenty-four hours it would be an official white Christmas in Walsall.

The kids were wrapped up in numerous layers of brightly coloured wintery clothing, their faces filled with the magical wonder of seeing so much snowfall. We hardly ever got snow much anymore, or if we did it wouldn't last and would be ruined by cars and too many footprints.

Christmas time was supposed to be magical and whilst pretentious pop-ups on social media showed better off families lavishing their precious offspring with ludicrous Pre-Christmas gifts we made do with simpler things, what we could afford.

We never really went away anywhere, just random days out during school holidays. The kids, well the oldest, our daughter Persephone, was almost seven which meant me and Steve hadn't been away together for at least that many years.

12 Days Of Christmas 2016

We didn't mind, we told ourselves that once our son, Patrick, was older, he was four, we would find away to go away. Having a horde of pets at our home and not really anyone else to care for them didn't give us that liberty anyway.

A few summers ago, whether it was a lottery funding or whatever, our local park, Walsall Arboretum, underwent a major overhaul and improvement. One of the new features, aside from a visitors centre and restaurant, had been the return of a land train and boating on the lake.

There used to be boats on the lake when I was a kid but they stopped it in the nighties because of some idiot kid falling in and drowning.

Last year, summer saw the fantastic return of boating on the lake, and the children's faces as they saw the seven swan pedalos gathered in a circle in the centre of the lake was a sight to behold.

Hell, even I was excited, probably just as much as they were.

Within the first day of the grand opening we had been on the pedalos twice. It was worth the money, and it really was beautiful, the boats so tranquil that the wildfowl would swim right alongside you like you were their mother.

When we saw the events list for the Christmas period it made the time even more special. Traditional carols with the Salvation Army brasses at the rebuilt bandstand, with mince pies and mulled wine. Candlelit walks, fairy lights twinkling in the trees at night and of course the muchly anticipated Seven Swans A-Swimming on Christmas Eve.

That's how we wound up first in the queue on Christmas Eve afternoon, we had booked a pedalo in October even though it had been pricey. It would be worth it for the kiddies. That's what Steve had said when we saw the flyer. I could tell he was just as interested in going but as ever he pretended to be modest and that he was doing it for all of us.

Even though it was really cold the water hadn't frozen, if this had have been the case then we would of course have been refunded and a carol service in the Visitor Centre would be the backup plan in that eventuality.

The park was naturally busy for a weekend, the luckily prepared people who could relax on the last day before the biggest day of the year were enjoying family time. Parents with babies, toddlers, students home from university, dogs to walk strolled around happily throwing breadcrumbs to the eager ducks and Canadian geese and just basking in their picturesque winter wonderland.

As we waited for our pedalo on the slatted wooden decking in the boathouse I couldn't help but smile at the other people who had pre-booked a boat for this joyous occasion. It was as though there was already an unspoken bond between us all, and we were all equally as excited.

I held on to Paddy's little mittened paw and thought how cute he looked in his furry brown wookie coat. Steve was overjoyed at all the Star Wars merchandise hitting the stores again, it meant he could dress the kids up in clothes that he secretly thought were cool even though the kids themselves had no interest whatsoever in the actual franchise.

Another family mirroring ours stood closeby, smiles and nods were exchanged whilst Persephone and their little girl, who seemed close in ages scrutinized one another's attire. Persephone thought it was the best thing in the world that this other girl was wearing the same fur-lined, hooded, Frozen coat as her but I could tell the other girl wasn't too happy. Well suck it up buttercup Seph rocks her coat so much better.

Their boy seemed just as uninterested in anyone as Paddy did, both of them holding onto the railings staring open-mouthed as a man on a red speedboat pulled the pedalos behind him from the centre of the lake.

Steve grinned at the father of the other family, he was always good at starting conversations. "You all ready for tomorrow?"

The other man rolled his eyes comically, "Yeah thank God, although knowing my luck I'll still have to traipse up to the petrol station tomorrow morning for something we've forgotten."

"Ha, yeah tell me about it." Steve said even though in my recollection he had never had to make such a venture on Christmas day. He pointed to the man's beanie, maroon with AVFC embroidered onto it, "I see you're a Villa fan."

With that the two men started waffling on about matches, fixtures and stereotypical football related nonsense whilst I felt forced to communicate with the other mother.

She was a fat woman, probably a bit older than me and I could tell the type who loathed anyone skinnier, younger or better looking than her. She smiled at me but only when she saw that I had noticed her scowl.

We began conversation but it was forced, Christmas plans, our roles as stereotypical wives, I was happy once the lifeguard arrived and a young couple started showing folk to their boats and issuing us with life jackets.

The lifeguard was bloody gorgeous, even though he would have looked more at home, and totally more acceptable to me, strutting his stuff on stage with the Chippendales or wearing red shorts and floppy blonde hair on Baywatch. He reminded me of the guy who played Flash Gordon in the classic film and I would have been as merciless as Ming if I had a chance at getting my hands on him.

Steve smirked when I pulled my subtle perv-face towards him, a crinkling of the mouth on one side and a nostril flare. We had an agreement, neither of us minded each other looking at other people, it was normal, but other than the occasional subtle ogling we had and always would be one hundred percent faithful.

Little Paddy was overwhelmed with the excitement of going in the pedalo during the snow and the added fact that our boat was number four, his favourite number. We got in our boat, me and Paddy in the rear, and Seph and Steve in the driving seats. Everyone else followed the boat attendants' orders, listened to safety rules and basic instructions and knew that once the bell was rung we needed to head back to the boat house.

So as we all sat there waiting for the boats to be filled the fit lifeguard stood on the deck drinking tea from a thermos flask. We didn't notice anything peculiar until after about half an hour on the lake.

Walsall was a busy town, it wasn't unusual for there to be sirens echoing around the streets at all hours. Most of the time though, as I mentioned before, all that would be forgotten once in the Arboretum. But that Christmas Eve afternoon there were dozens of them. Naturally, wrapped up in our lovely surroundings, we weren't that bothered about it, the noise had registered with us but didn't take up much more of our attention.

We circled the lake, our breath billowing before us, the wildfowl seemed exceptionally friendly, swimming close enough to touch if we reached out far enough.

I could see the lifeguard standing by the red speedboat, far off on the other side of the lake, talking heatedly to the boat attendants. His arms gesticulating wildly and pointing out towards the main entrance.

That was when the crunches, clunks and smashing of metal and glass began to infiltrate the park as the cars, lorries and buses outside on the busy road started crashing into one another.

"Jesus Christ, sounds like one hell of a pile up out there." Steve said stopping pedaling to listen to the cacophony coming from outside the red walls.

Endless car horns, more metallic crunches and sirens, so many sirens.

"Daddy, what's happening?" Seph said looking up at her father eyes wide with worry.

Steve pushed his glasses up his nose and grinned, "just people rushing about getting all flustered because it's Christmas Eve."

The other six boats were dotted about in various points across the lake.

Morbid curiosity got the better of the old couple, I watched their boat move towards a stretch of the lake adjacent to the red bricked clock tower that stood over the entrance. Groups of milling park visitors began to flock towards the arched opening to investigate the sounds of carnage.

"People are so bloody nosy." Steve said disgustedly and pumped his feet up and down on the pedals and propelled us through the black water. "Come on Seph, let's see if we can get this round Duck Island."

Seph cheered and stomped her Wellington booted feet in time with her dad's. Duck Island was our nickname for a small wooded island just off the side of the lake, a few circular piers had been built around that corner to make it more picturesque and so people could enjoy the age old pastime of feeding the ducks. A narrow channel ran between the island and the mainland of the park, about as wide as two cars nose to tail. It was obvious the boat would fit Steve just wanted to show off his steering skills and keep the kids occupied.

Paddy poked his lower lip out sadly in the direction of the entrance and said, "Nee-nahs." His word for anything vehicular with a wailing, flashing light.

I put my arm around him and instinctively squeezed him too tightly when the sound of screaming drowned out the noises on the road.

Steve stopped pedaling and I turned round in the seat and squinted towards the entrance where a lot of the people in the park had congregated. The shrieking got louder and something came into the park. The people surrounding the entrance moved backwards as one like a Mexican wave, the group circling outwards like ripples on water after a stone's drop. The crowd of people stampeded away from whatever had come into the park, running like their lives depended on it.

Steve and Seph had managed to get the boat halfway along the channel between the land and Duck Island, so we were close to the iron railings at the top of the lake's bank when the fleeing visitors ran by.

What I saw, was something from a clichéd horror film. There were people amongst the crowds attacking each other, using hands, feet and teeth as weapons. They were quick, quicker than they should be. One man I saw was clinically obese and yet he pounded after another man like a long distant runner, his fat belly wobbling out beneath his jumper and pushing his trousers down. I watched as he grabbed the closest person to him and forced them up against the iron railing. The person who he was attacking tried their best to defend themselves but the fat man was like a wild animal. He clobbered the person, I couldn't make out the gender, picked them up in a bearhug and brought them down heavily onto the spiked railings. One of the spikes skewered the person through the chest and whilst other attackers like the fat man chased down potential victims, the fat man tore frantically at the spiked person's clothing and continued into their flesh.

"Zombies." Seph said breaking our silent shock, "like on The Walking Dead."

Nobody said anything, Steve just stared and concentrated on manoeuvring the pedalo back into the more open expanse of the lake. I clung to Paddy for dear life.

I saw the occupants of the other boats staring at the insane riot around us and knew our faces matched theirs.

The attackers, infected or as Seph said, zombies, spread throughout the running people like wildfire, their speed unnatural.

Steve yelled at Seph to pedal as some of the stragglers noticed us not far from the shore line. Something was up with their coordination, they just ran at the railings and toppled over rather than climb over.

I hugged Paddy closer and told my husband and daughter to hurry, a few of the infected had righted themselves and were now sloshing through the water towards us.

Even though where they were at the boathouse was pretty safe and secure the sexy lifeguard drew attention to himself and the young attendants by calling out over the lake on a megaphone.

"Make your way to the centre of the lake as soon as possible." He repeated himself twice.

The infected horde who were quickly overthrowing the park visitors, hunting in packs and individually, began flocking in the direction of the boathouse.

As Steve and Seph got the boat out of the narrow channel, the infected people in the water had just vanished beneath the surface, I saw the person who had been impaled on the railings push themself off the green spikes and run in relentlessly towards the boathouse.

It was exactly what Seph had said, zombies.

I couldn't believe the speed in which the infection spread. In the space of half an hour all of the inhabitants in the park aside from us on the pedalos and those in the boathouse had transformed into flesh hungry killing machines. More and more groups of infected swarmed through the gates like ants, alerted maybe to the sounds of death-cries, screaming, at teeth tearing meat.

The other boats and ours floated in a circle in the centre of the lake, all eyes were on the boathouse, in a way our last hope. Paddy refused to get his face from under my arm and I wasn't going to force him. The kids in the other boat, the matching family who we had spoken to before getting in the boats, were wailing like banshees. Their parents did little to comfort them. Everyone else was silent.

Within the first five minutes of getting the boats to the centre of the lake almost everyone's mobile phones came out as people dialled for help.

The people that got through to some authorities looked horrified, or laughed incredulously at the replies they were given.

Try and keep safe and hidden until help arrived, when that would be could not be determined.

Steve hung up the phone and swore under his breath. "I'm sure they'll sort this out soon." He offered Seph a smile but I knew it hadn't fooled her at all.

All around the lake the infected loomed, bumping into one another sniffing each other like animals. Any lucky uninfected were taken down instantly, a frenzied race for the infected to pull apart and eat before they too got up and walked.

"We're fucked man." The young Indian man, said smacking his palm against the pedalo.

"Don't curse, there are children present." The man who I presumed was his father said from the seat beside him.

"He's right though," Came a voice from one of the other boats, the boy in the young couple, floppy long fringe and nose piercing. His girlfriend sobbing on his shoulder. "Look," He pointed a gloved finger towards the boathouse, it was surrounded by a large group of the infected. The hot lifeguard was handing out life jackets to the two attendants and they were hurriedly packing stuff into the red speedboat. The horde were reaching through the high iron railings, too dumb to find a way through. Though the fence was high and strong the sheer number of infected pushing against it began to topple the railings, the iron poles ploughing through and lifting up the soil.

12 Days Of Christmas 2016

We sat there completely useless to help, held our breaths as the fences finally gave way and the infected swarmed the boathouse.

Steve spotted something behind me and shouted at Seph to pedal.

The boat with the four nerdy men was racing towards the opposite side of the lake by the entrance. It was clear. The horde had overrun the boathouse and those guys were utilising the distraction to chance an escape.

The others soon caught on and like some novelty boat race the remaining five pedalos followed suit. I daren't look back, I couldn't face seeing those poor people being ripped to shreds.

I was amazed at how speedily those four guys got their boat across the lake. Steve was red-faced and panting with the physical exertion of pedaling with all his might and yelling at Seph to go faster even though she was petrified and exhausted.

The Indian family weren't far behind them, closely followed by the young couple. As was probably expected the older couple brought up the rear.

The closer we got to the entrance the more I thought we were going to make it, but I could also see more of the devastation outside the park. Vehicles on fire, the mother of all pile-ups.

The nerd boat didn't stop until the chest and neck of the swan had bumped up and onto the bank unending the pedalo and knocking the two guys in the back seat into the cold water. There was no loyalty towards friends there, the two at the front leapt from the boat and vaulted over the railings before their companions had even begun to wade to the shore.

The first man made it out of the park, at least I think he did as the next second a hulking great shadow filled the light arched entrance and a red,white and blue double decker bus came grinding to a halt.

The force of the collision obliterated the top deck of the bus with the lower ramming into and through the entrance whilst the top crushed against the red brick clock tower.

I don't know what happened to the second guy out of the boat, I presume he was killed by the bus.

When the bus collided the front windows smashed and we could make out the passengers spilling out of the broken windscreen.

They too were infected.

The two men who had fallen in the water were frozen waist deep in the lake. After the shock of the bus crash sank in and the infected passengers started climbing from the wreckage they saw no other option than to try and swim towards the nearest pedalo, theirs being moored.

The Indian family shook their heads, the older son shouting obscenities at the two men. All I could understand was the father of the group repeatedly shaking his head and shouting, "No room, no room."

They turned the boat around and headed towards us.

The infected had scaled the railings and were splashing through the shallow water after the two men.

One of the swimmers was far ahead, a strong swimmer, despite their frosty reception he grabbed the side of the Indian family's pedalo and tried to pull himself on board. I had a horrific image of him throwing one of them overboard.

What actually happened was just as bad.

The older boy, the one who spewed bad language struck out with his foot. I saw the swimmer's nose explode like a red paint splat and him fall backwards into the water where the lifejacket kept him afloat.

His friend caught up with him and hooked an arm across his chest.

"Over here." At last somebody tried to help the two men. It was the boy from the young couple. He reached his arm outwards towards the swimmers.

Behind all this the passengers from the bus were all in the water but thankfully whatever was infecting them prevented them or maybe made them forget such skills as swimming.

The swimmer who had rescued his friend helped lift his friend into the pedalo and climbed in afterwards.

One by one the infected's heads vanished below the surface.

A loud motor from behind made us all turn, I had forgotten about the hot lifeguard and the boat attendants. The red speedboat skipped across the lake, the lifeguard standing at the rear of the boat controlling the motor whilst the young couple crouched near the front, clinging to a rope that ran around the boat's edge.

The boathouse was swarmed with the infected, they wandered up and down the decking half distracted by us all in the boats and half distracted by the noise that the ducks and geese had begun to make.

Some of the infected people had made it to Duck Island and were clumsily snatching for the ducks and geese. The birds, some of the big ones like the swans and geese had nests on there and were naturally aggressive protecting their eggs. But they were smarter than the infected people, they knew mankind was a more deadly predator and that if their usual honks, pecks and hisses didn't keep potential attackers at bay there was nothing more they could do.

The birds reluctantly surrendered their island, I was happy none of them got hurt.

We grouped together in the centre, the lifeguard had risked his and the boat attendants' lives by filling his vessel with as many useful items that they had at the boathouse before it became overrun.

When it got dark and the temperature dropped he handed out torches and blankets. There wasn't enough to go around but once a couple of the men had shown bravado by suggesting that the women and kids had priority the rest agreed to do the same.

I huddled in the back of our boat with Paddy and Seph. Steve sat in front with the torch.

Nothing much was said in the first few hours of settling in the centre of the lake, we all tried the emergency services again but there was an automated message whenever anyone got through.

There was nothing to eat and nothing to drink, and it was getting colder and colder.

So we all sat in the dark, the red speedboat and it's occupants had taken leadership. The young kids, ours and the other family's had finally managed to get to sleep. We started talking mostly to focus on something other than the mournful wailing coming from the infected that surrounded us. Dusk, and the lights and moans from the park had brought even more infected people to the park. Even in this seemingly apocalyptic event it was a popular destination.

"I'm Rick," The lifeguard spoke from the dark, he had a broad Australian accent. A female voice beside him told us her name was Sarah.

"Mike," said the other boat attendant.

We could hardly see one another but had had the time to memorise people's whereabouts.

"We're Jack and Vera," said the old man to our left, I smiled instantly thinking of the Duckworths in Coronation Street.

"Andrew," The young man said, "and my girlfriend's Laura." The young man shone a torch beneath his face for a second.

"Rhys," said the man with the busted nose, all the lifeguard had been able to offer him in the way of first aid was a wad of gauze.

"Jonathan," Came the voice of Rhys's rescuer beside him.

"Ahmed." The father of the Indian family begun, "my two sons are Tobias and Muhammad, and my wife Iqra."

We introduced ourselves.

"What's the point eh?" said a male voice that hadn't been introduced yet, it had to be the father of the other family like ours.

"What do you mean buddy?" Rick the lifeguard asked.

"Well unless your surname's Grimes then we're fucked." The man said.

I don't know whether or not the lifeguard got the reference to the popular zombie programme as he made no comment acknowledging it. "There's no harm in introducing one another mate. Sure, we're in a pretty shitty predicament right now but things might start looking up in the morning."

The man laughed bitterly, "It's freezing out here, we have no food, no drink, not enough blankets. We'll be lucky to make it til the morning."

Even though he was only saying what the rest of us were thinking it was still hard to hear it.

"I don't know what else to suggest mate. But just in case I need to shout your name out to stop one of those things over there from chowing down on one of your kids could you at least tell us what you're called?"

The other man sighed, "I'm Terry, my wife's Charlotte and the kids are George and May."

"Thanks," Rick said from the confines of his boat.

The night time was terrible, the cold unbearable. The four of us huddled together around Steve. Steve's a big man, always warm and cosy to cuddle up to, it was weird to see him cold enough to shiver. We grouped together like a family of penguins protecting their young, keeping every inch of ourselves hidden from the elements.

All night those bloody things paced backwards and forwards around the lake's edge, moaning and groaning like they were somehow communicating in caveman grunts.

I was woken by the screams of the young lady, Laura I think her name was. She was sat with her gloved hands over her pale face staring in the direction of the bandstand.

I looked in that direction and reacted the same except I forced my hand over my mouth as to not disturb the kids or make any more noise.

Surrounding us was a thick white expanse of ice. The lake had frozen solid.

Ducks padded back and forth, sliding about comically, well it would have been funny, endearing, except Laura's shriek had reminded the wandering infected that we were still here.

Laura's boyfriend Andrew hugged her fiercely and pulled her into his chest, partly to comfort, partly to silence her but it was too late.

The others began to wake up groggily, the effects of a night outside in freezing temperatures had obviously taken its toll on them. Lots of hand rubbing and jiggling about to try and get some life back into their extremities.

The first of the infected stepped onto the ice and instantly fell on its arse, it kept slipping and sliding about as it attempted to get back up. In the end it flipped over onto its front and started crawling towards us like a baby.

Rick, the hot lifeguard, searched in the speedboat for anything that could be used as a weapon but there was nothing.

"Okay, everyone, we have to do something. Any ideas?" He shouted, panic in his voice for the first time as we could only watch as the infected slid, staggered and crawled across the frozen surface.

Everyone was shouting at once, eyes darting this way and that trying to find a solution. It was then I saw the older couple in their boat, hand in hand and frozen to death. I knew that it wasn't the time to get upset over this but I pointed it out to Rick and the others.

I didn't point it out as a possible solution to our problem, and what they did next appalled me and still haunts me more than all the other barbarity I've been witness to.

Rick put a booted foot onto the ice and pressed down hard testing how thick it was. "We need to break the ice around the boats, the lake is too deep for them to do much if they go under." Keeping one hand on the boats in case the ice cracked he carefully walked towards the old couple's pedalo.

While the rest of us kicked at the ice with our heels he paused for a few seconds before the old couple as though saying a prayer. Then he prized the couple apart and lifted the old lady up in his arms like all the heroes do in the movies. I thought it was sweet that he was going to keep their bodies safe, that he was going to put Jack and Vera in his boat. I was wrong.

Rick lifted the old woman's body high above his head and as the realisation of what he was going to do set in I screamed for him to stop. He hurled the old lady's corpse like it weighed nothing towards the fast approaching monsters. A large crack spider-webbed all around where the body struck the ice and it skidded across the slippery surface and knocked several infected over like skittles. They were on the woman within seconds, tearing away her clothes to get to her flesh.

The ice had weakened where Vera had hit and sharp gunshots echoed about as it began to crack.

We couldn't help but cheer as the section of ice where the body was being devoured collapsed and a dozen of them vanished into the black water. Maybe that had been his plan, to get enough of them in one small place that it would break through.

The infected were coming from all around us, we needed to break the ice surrounding us. All the adults were out of the pedalos holding on and desperately jumping up and down on the ice.

Rick lifted Jack up, his spectacles dropping by to the ice. He held the skinny dead man by the ankles and used his frozen corpse like a fucking sledgehammer. Jack's dead skull thunked against the ice, the contents of his pockets flying everywhere. He did it again and his head broke and made the most disgusting noise ever, I puked onto the ice.

Rick struck the ice again and again and finally broke through. He was like a man possessed, covered in the congealed blood and gore of a dead body he was using as a hammer. It was working.

Steve and Terry began to kick the edges of the hole Rick had made, the ice finally giving way. I tried my best to cover the children's eyes even though it was hopeless, they were hysterical.

The infected were still closing in on us. In places where the early morning sun had warmed enough they fell through but there were too many.

The Indian family saved our lives.

They had been mostly huddled together whispering throughout this and I feel bad now for suspecting them of working on a plan to double cross us.

The father Ahmed pushed his boy into the arms of the young couple and muttered something.

Then the mother and father and eldest son hugged and shouted out something in Urdu or whatever, like, and I hate to say it, you hear about the terrorists shouting before they bombed somewhere.

The three family members ran in opposite directions yelling as hard and as loud as they could, waving their hands above their heads to cause as much disturbance as possible.

The effect this had on the shuffling multitudes was instant. It was like they had woken up and realised there was more food to be had.

They climbed over the railings at literally poured onto the ice.

We grabbed the kids and ran towards the less crowded part of the lake edge hoping and praying that the ice was strong enough.

It's funny, whenever I've previously dared step onto ice I've always taken small dainty steps, expecting to slip over at any opportunity. But when running for dear life across a surface that may or may not be strong enough to hold your weight it's surprising how reckless you are.

We bounded across the ice, if we slipped we kept on running, Steve had Seph in his arms, I had a screaming Paddy in mine. I think the others were behind us.

I chanced a glance over my shoulder at just the right moment to see the infected pile on top of the Indian lady like vultures on a carcass. The father of the family had made it to Duck Island and was beating the infected away with a thick piece of branch, a flurry of feathers engulfed him like a snowstorm as the birds fled in every direction.

The grown up son had somehow miraculously made it to the boathouse and was trying to pull himself up onto the tiled roof when he was yanked down into the cluster of the ravenous mouths below him.

Steve shoulder barged a couple of the straggling infected out of the way, his twenty stone bulk no match for anything that got in his way. The others followed behind us, the other family carrying their children, the young couple hand in hand, the two nerds behind them followed by the boat attendants and Rick who had the sobbing little Indian boy in his arms.

Steve was amazing, he cleared a path amongst the few wanderers that came into his path, charging like a rhino.

We were almost at the edge of the lake, no more than twenty feet when Steve dropped through the lake in one fluid motion. One second he was there the next gone, even though I saw every detail as if it took forever. His right foot slamming down in front of him and sinking straight through the ice. The wide eyed expression of fear as he went downwards. And the instinct reaction to thrust Seph as hard as he could in front of him before as he fell.

My scream matched my daughter's as she skated across the ice on her backside and rolled onto the bank.

I sped up and dropped Paddy to the bank before rushing to the jagged hole.

There was no sign of him at all. Before I knew it the two nerdy men had grabbed me under the armpits and were hoisting me onto the embankment.

We had to go, Rick said nodding behind him to the demonic horde chasing him across the ice.

Why? Why did the ice hold enough for those bastards but not my husband?

If it hadn't been for my children I would have given up there and then.

But I didn't.

We went to the entrance of the arboretum with natural caution. Just over a dozen of us, we were freezing, thirsty and starving hungry, but we couldn't stop. We can never stop, our fight is endless. We can never stop, not even on Christmas Day.

12 Days Of Christmas 2016

Six Geese Laying- Ezekiel Jacobs

I DON'T KNOW WHY today was different from the last few years, I just, I dunno, had a feeling.

A worn path wove through the long grass of the shrapnel field, a rarely used entrance to the park. It dropped you off a close to playground where me and some kid that one of my aunts was babysitting played together. Never did get his name.

Now they had ripped out the fun things to play on for tame objects with ropes and safety nets, this whole new generation were pussies.

I passed the manor that was in this park, now a glorified gift shop, slid through the busking lane where they all hang out, and made my way to the quiet area of the park.

Down here there was a pond, a pond that on first glance was just a small C of water amid a bunch of overgrown trees. Thing is, not knowing for sure if anyone other than the park rangers knew, if you pushed past a bunch of trees and bushes there was so much more to the pond than most were aware of. This area was desolate, again, since not many knew about it. I always wondered why since there was a gap in the trees to the main road.

A tree trunk that had been carved into a head, a sculpture from a bygone time. Covered in cobwebs and still sporting the rusted screws for its pupils. I came to see this thing as my own personal item in this area, since it must have been created long before nature reclaimed the spot.

I filled a coke bottle full of rum, not because I was a depressive alcoholic, it wasn't because I didn't respect the prohibition of drinking in public. I was not having a good week and needed it. I was not a stupid drunk, I was capable of being a normal when needed be.

The C of water turned into a big loop in this hidden area, making the shape of your generic train set or race car track. It was in this secluded area that I was truly at peace.

Downing half the bottle within ten minutes, I sat there with this wild idea of selling the home and simply living in this small haven. The pain in my fingers dulled, the strives of my situation faded, the drink removed all my troubles.

Maybe I was an alcoholic. Maybe what I feel is right is wrong, who's to tell? Everybody else I guess. I sat there, on a bench covered in vines, glugging away as I did my daily contemplation of my life as it was now. Traffic could be heard from the main road, and the odd sound of the kids playing in the playground could be heard, but all I could hear was the voices from my past.

Ever since I could remember I spent every second of time off school to be with my Grandma. She was the best. She was my father's mother, her and all that side of my family lived in Yorkshire. Even though the two hour train ride to and from her house was the worst form of torture for the parent of a fidgety kid like me, it was all worth it in my eyes if it meant I got to see her. Enough sitcoms and movies showed me that Grandmothers were often crazy and eccentric, nutty so-and-so's that most wouldn't allow to look after their children. But my Grandma was nothing like that, far from it. Okay, she may have been the kind to always have a cigarette on the go (Black Super King, I'll never forget), and have an unhealthy obsession for Neil Diamond, but besides that she was the coolest Grandma any child could wish for.

I still remember when that lady from One Foot In The Grave became the figurehead for a bunch of old-age adverts. From the front room, watching 24/7 cartoons on her satellite television that I didn't have back home, every time I heard the advert start I knew what was coming... and all I did was smile. I shouldn't have, because back home I would have gotten scolded hard. I swear, now that I'm older, I can safely say my mom was a right bitch.

Anyway, when those adverts came on I heard all manner of words used to tell someone to, politely, get lost come out her mouth. Then, as always, I'd hear her call my name to pick up all the stuff she'd thrown at her TV. I was too young to understand why she did it, she may have been doing it to make me laugh for all I knew.

They were good times, and unlike the bad times the good ones end far too quickly. Age can't be stopped just because you think you feel young. A genetic problem within her family, and also my mother's side which bodes well for me, huh? Is arthritis. Maybe it's paranoia or maybe it's because I crack my knuckles every chance I get, but I sometimes feel like the tingling in my fingers is it starting to affect me. One thing I know for sure is that I inherited my mother's side when it came to my hair. My father's side of the family literally were stone grey by the time they were thirty. I was almost there and even though there was no grey in sight, not even the cool kind of grey that Reed Richards has, I was for sure going bald. Fuck!

Her arthritis was bad, real bad. Her bed became her chair, her seat at the dining table, and eventually her grave.

I didn't see it then but now I understand the smile she gave me was her thanking God that I was there to spend time with her. I just wish I'd been a bit more aware at the time... to prove what I mean: I was a kid who was disappointed with the end of Back to the Future. Now, it brings me to tears when Doc and Marty say their goodbyes to each other, but back then I was angry that all Marty got after that was a photo... I was an idiot of a child who expected a toy to play with, not a priceless bit of proof that the river of time was something that could possibly be travelled both ways.

I live with the regret everyday that I could've been a better grandchild to her, along with the embarrassment with not understanding the power of one of the best trilogies of all time.

So, yeah, time progressed as harshly as it always does, and her ability to animate herself worsened. Then, when I was back at home with my mother she told me the reality of the situation. I guess my obliviousness was to my advantage that day, seeing as how it saved me from breaking down at the time.

Then... after I visited her in hospital one time a few years later, during which she promised so much, I woke up the next day to see my mother and sister at my bedroom door with red eyes. On that day my life became a numb mess – the worst had taken place. The only person who mattered in my life was gone. Free of her own physical pains, but burdening me with them on a mental level in their place.

12 Days Of Christmas 2016

The one thing I was unaware of at the time was the sudden interest she took up during those bad years with geese. Ornaments, pictures, even a frame containing photos of a bunch of real geese appeared in the front room. This was clear signs of age affecting her mind, but this replica of my grandma that returned from hospital was tainted by something, underlying malevolence.

The home of a hoarder was what remained, my Grandma slowly transitioned between child and adult. Geese everywhere, stuffed toys from charity shops with mismatched eyes, tea towels with flocks a flight in their V formation.

She would sit in that chair of hers, cigarette glued to the sagging corner of her toothless maw, a witch's cackle would shake her jowls and she would sing.

Christmas is coming,

The goose is getting fat,

Please put a penny in the old man's hat.

If you haven't got a penny,

A ha'penny will do,

If you haven't got that,

12 Days Of Christmas 2016

Then God bless you

The cackle would escalate into a mucus rich, wheezing cough that would have her thumping at her chest like a gorilla.

This was not my grandma.

And yet, I made a stupid yet semi-justifiable choice.

After I left school, not doing too good and earning a pittance on the nearby college's work-experience program, an opportunity came to me. I wasn't the most social of people, and even though a job in care seemed too cringe worthy, if it was to become the carer of my own Grandma, wasn't that a job I'd be perfect for?

Crossing new boundaries, having to shower and change her wasn't the most lucrative items on the job list that I was now in charge of, but it brought comfort to her and the family. No uncaring asshole would need to rush through the mundane job of washing another crusty old fart just so they could get away as fast as they could. It would being taken care of by a member of the family.

I got to live with my Grandma from then on. Which meant I got away from my insane mother.

12 Days Of Christmas 2016

Those two and a half years were, no doubt, the best years of my life. By far. Despite her descent into senile dementia.

The aunts and uncles, her children and their own children, did the minimum, and I was always thankful for their help. The worst happened, I was fired.

My grandma died.

The night she died I remember having the shit scared out of me.

Whether something had spooked them in the nearby park, or, for all I knew, the bloody things were nocturnal, I do not know. But I lay in bed, contemplating my future now the worst had happened, I heard the honking. Far off at first, I thought it was a lone bird scared, or maybe warding off a night time predator, but it's raucous call was joined by another and another. They got louder and louder until I honestly thought they were inside the house. I could hear the beating of their wings as the flock passed over the house, in the dark night sky. A vision of a spectral flock of my grandma's strange and sudden senile obsession flooded my head. A ghostly herald of long-necked birds flying over her house to carry her soul on the tips of white-tipped spirit wings.

12 Days Of Christmas 2016

When I found her that morning there had been crumpled note in her dead hand. In her jittery handwriting. Don't let them take the geese.

My father, a person I'd never seen before was coming to the funeral, and my aunts and uncles were all asking if it was okay with me if he came.

I agreed.

I didn't want him to come so I could demand to know why he walked out on my mother mere days after I was born, I just wanted to see him. All I had was a family photo of the lot of them to go on, and that was taken long before I was born.

We talked, we laughed, I had no ill-thoughts about him, it was fine.

After the funeral we all had drinks, played all her favourite Neil Diamond songs. Apart from the one time I got caught drinking alcopops in school, this was the first time I got proper drunk. Everyone, even the other carers that helped with the installation of handles and implements that made her life easy were there, even the one with the cute face and huge boobs.

Proud moments took a wide berth for what came next. Her will left everything to her children, even my father, to the others dislike. I understand his awkwardness during that meal now. I thought it was because meeting me after all this time, but it was because he'd shamed the rest of the family due to his abandonment of my mother. Still, though I'm now an adult and aware of things, I don't blame him. I don't even know if he's alive or dead at this point, but I still wish I'd gotten him to stay.

I was fine with her children getting what they were given, but when it came to one thing I was the one to stick my dick in the works and make things complicated.

The house she lived in. I wanted to keep it.

The issue went down with as much grace as a cement block in a washing machine. In the end, with a bad taste in my mouth after hearing all of the family's opinion of my choice, I won. I was allowed to keep the house and continue to pay the bills off of my wages at a job I'd gotten in the nearby corner shop.

Naturally her children sold everything in it, I was left with the bare minimum, useless items of no value, even to thrift stores.

And the geese.

A rusty old metal drum had sat slowly disintegrating ever since I can remember in my grandma's backyard. I loaded all of the unsightly combustible goose paraphernalia into it and took pleasure in watching the horrid things burn away.

Her family shunned me for what I'd done, and despite the small efforts afterwards they severed all contact.

I was free of my mother, but now unable to hang with my father's side of family, the main reason I'd chosen to stay in the first place. Talk about out of the frying pan and into another frying pan.

And now, traversing my mid-twenties, I was alone for the first time in my life.

My mother shrugged her shoulders at my decision and the rest didn't want anything to do with me. Even my great aunt, the sister of my Grandma, despite her efforts to aid me in maintaining the home that meant so much to all of them, kept her distance. She wasn't totally against me, it was that she wanted to stay in the rest of the family's good graces. We talked about it, about a lot of things, and I didn't blame her.

In my heart I was doing the right thing, it is what she would have wanted. At least apart from me going against her dying wish.

Not like it matters now, huh?

All this stuff, all these memories, replay through my head every single morning, when I wake up to that lonely house.

12 Days Of Christmas 2016

I got up and showered, had breakfast and got dressed. I spent my usual amount of time looking out the bathroom window at the playground beyond the back gate where me and a bunch of friends long ago would play, gazing further to the trees that were not as tall as they used to be anymore.

All I did was what I've been doing for the past four years at the sight of it all, I sighed.

The morning light illuminated the dust that lingered in the air, each and every single speck. Nothing besides the small corner of my Grandmother's bedroom was any different than what it was when she died. I hadn't the money or desire to redecorate, as though a part of me knew that it shouldn't be mine. White silhouettes, clean spots on the nicotine stained wallpaper, where the China geese flew never seemed to vanish beneath the dust and grime.

I managed to worm a three-day weekend from work this month, and this was day one. Slumping into her old chair, I flicked on the TV to catch the morning cartoons. They were all crap these days, but it sure beat having to look around the room at the spaces where the geese had been.

Don't let them take the geese.

12 Days Of Christmas 2016

What was it about fucking geese anyway? Her fixation had been so sudden. Hell, I even remember her telling me once what goose tasted like. Why, if someone loved something so damn much, why would they willingly consume it?

That was why I was going to go to the secret spot Grandma had told me about today, the one she talked about so much during those last few weeks. "Don't forget to feed the geese lad, when I'm gone. You must remember to feed the geese."

I was told it was because of the strong painkillers that she took, it made her talkative about random things, but today was the day I'd go see the geese.

With each mouthful of drink the volume lowered, making me drink more, and with each gulp the heat from the sun became colder. Maybe I was drunk, or maybe Yorkshire was finally going to have a proper winter this year.

I looked at the Tupperware box of ham sandwiches I'd brought and wondered why I had bothered. To feed the geese? I, for sure, wasn't going to eat them. Drink and food don't mix for me. Plus, a new noise that had become apparent was making me feel more sick than any amount of drink could bring on, even though they were the reason of my visit.

Geese, not imaginary or spectral, real ones, swam from under the overgrown bush and into my sanctuary. I turned to see them thrashing about excitedly in the water, pearls of water rolling off their naturally water resistant plumage.

I sneered at the white things as they glided along the stagnant water, and wished for a rock instead of stale sandwiches.

Geese… ornaments and pictures had been everywhere in that house. I had hated them with a passion. They had emphasised things were changing, symbols of the disintegration of my grandma's mind.

She removed all other decorations for her own bird-themed ones. I cried for few nights the time she filled the house with birds.

It was my uncle who took me for Chinese that told me she was just 'confused', and likely the geese were something significant to her earlier years, or perhaps maybe she thought they were some kind of saviour to get her to heaven.

She had been a devout Christian. Church had been a regulatory requirement, I had no problems with that. I wasn't a rebel as a kid. But I don't remember anything about geese.

A bridge, if you could call it that, connected the mainland to an island in the pond most birds around here slept during the night. I watched the geese that had emerged hop across it to get into this portion of the pond and I laughed enough to startle them.

Noisy little bastards.

I downed another mouthful as I watched a trio of the birds bob into the murky water before hopping onto the shore to waddle about. I slumped down as I watched.

They were to blame.

Everything in my life then was of my own doing, there was no way out when it was like this.

As I watched the geese that my grandma had grown fond of during her late years play about on land, I relived treasured memories shared with her.

I was brought to tears as my thoughts turned to carrying her coffin down the aisle of the church as her favourite Neil Diamond song played.

Fucking life and it's shit rules. Why give her arthritis?! And dementia on top of that? Why make her heart stop?! She was a devout Christian!

"No!" I said aloud, all the geese raising their heads and looking towards me, "you had to take her!"

The drink had taken me quickly, which was a rare thing, so I thanked the God that had taken my grandma that no one was around to hear me say that.

Cars passed by and the noises the geese made filled the silence as I sat there wiping my eyes. I cursed myself for another day of not being able to get over the past. I even gave a nearby goose the finger because it had gotten too close to me as I sat wallowing in self-pity.

The dumb creature bobbed its head from left to right and gazed at me with beaded peppercorn eyes. It must be great to be a docile creature. Not having to worry about jobs and money, regarding the loss of related geese with a mere shrug.

"My grandma said she always came here," I told the nearby one, "loved you little pricks enough to donate all her other antiques. The ones I loved. Now I'm here… so show me what good you are!"

The trio of geese that waddled about near the bridge to the island they had sprung from pecked about while giving me and each other odd glances.

The geese did their thing, pecking around and whatnot, but when one of them squatted and shat out an egg I focused on them solely. That was not something thing I expected to see. Seriously, the thing just bent its little legs and plopped out an egg… a real one. This was no cartoon bouncy white egg, it was a gross yellow egg speckled with red stains.

The other geese surrounded her, a female laying an egg, that's logic, honking and hissing. I sat there watching all this take place.

I'll admit that I'd never seen geese lay before.

The three others all surrounded the new mother and all honked in unison, their necks thrusting upward like trumpet fanfare.

I blinked a few times to make sure that this was really happening. They were singing. Not just making noise because they were annoying birds and that's what annoying birds do all day, but because one of them had laid an egg.

The new parent turned and nudged the egg with its bill. With painstaking care, the goose rolled the egg with its beak across the little bridge towards the island in the middle of the pond.

I wondered whether this was some natural ritualistic thing in birds. I was clueless when it came to things that were outside my interest.

The others followed behind in some bizarre parade. Absent-minded, I opened my lunchbox and began digging into my sandwiches.

A solitary goose stayed behind and stood guard. It was silent and ignored by the others as they disappeared into the overgrown bushes of the little island. It just hung around while the rest seemingly cheered for the new parent.

When the happy family escaped my blurred perception, I focused on that lone goose. It wasn't like there was anything to identify it or anything, let's face it, they all look alike, right? It stood there, silent, looking around.

I looked at the coke bottle and found it with only a few gulps left. Not like I recall drinking that much, but I never concentrated on how much I drank?

A flashback prepared to do take over my vision as the alcohol weighted my eyelids. I was ready to be taken on another ride into darkness, but on the cusp of consciousness I heard my grandma's voice whisper, "don't forget to feed the geese lad, when I'm gone."

I jolted awake, back to secluded spot, my sight returned to that one goose that stood apart from the flock.

In its mouth was a shiny object, but not just any shiny object. "You little bastard!" I slurred and pushed myself up, "those are my keys!"

Yeah, the duck-thing had my keys. I didn't recall them falling out of my pocket, but this was a situation that required no back-tracking. The bottle opener shaped like a shark was the give-away, it seriously had the keys to my grandma's house in its mouth.

"Hey!" I shouted, tripping over my own feet to get to the goose. "Feathery shit," I said, as it looked towards me. "Give me that."

It made a noise and then hopped onto the bridge and waddled towards the island.

In its beak was the only means of entering my grandma's home. Like it or not, I needed to get them back. The goose, which was one of those brown and black ones, hopped onto the island and fled into the overgrown foliage.

Little sod. I was determined it wasn't going to get away. I was an articulate drunk and didn't think twice when it came to traversing the thin bridge between here and that overgrown island. I pranced across it with ease and crawled through the initial bush to discover a tower of dirt.

I shook my head to try and rid myself of the rum's influence, but it was no good. I had to close one eye to spot the goose that had my keys climb up and out of sight over the summit of this dirt mountain.

Not one to be outmatched by Sunday dinner, I ignored my own little dislike for dirty fingernails and clawed my way up this cone of mud to reclaim what was mine. What else was I going to do, phone somebody? Who? Who would help me? Would the RSPCA for birds come out for a incident of goose robbery?

The dizziness came in handy for when I reached the summit of this hill and discovered that this was no mere pile of dirt. It was a crater, a miniature hollow mountain, with a certain surprise waiting for my eyes in its centre.

I told myself it had to be the drink, had to be, because as I looked down into this hollow mountain I saw a giant pile of white shapes.

Eggs.

Dozens and dozens of eggs, all in a heaped pile. I swallowed hard as I saw what lined the huge nest. There were no twigs or leaves to keep the pile together. The half-eaten carcasses and skeletons of dead wildlife kept the pile in its place. Dogs, cats, the odd squirrel, and indecipherable varieties of rodent.

If I had been more lucid I may have heaved at the sight of all this, in this state of drunkenness though I took all this reasonably well. I was just more interested in reclaiming my keys.

I spotted the goose, the one with my keys, on the other side of the pile of eggs. Then another came into view, gazing at the pile, then another, and another. Six, six in all, stood around this pile, each atop the rotted corpse of a half-eaten animal. What in the hell was this?!

12 Days Of Christmas 2016

They all honked in unison, their webbed feet slapping, the limp flesh beneath them acted like a drum skin.

I watched from my spot as they all looked up towards the summit of the pile to where a seventh goose emerged. This one was a goose, a proper goose. The goose settled itself atop the pile and let out a loud honk. It was pure white with an orange bill. I shook my head in disbelief, it wore something. I tried to identify what exactly was on the big goose's back, thinking it had trapped itself in a plastic carrier bag or some other piece of litter.

Unbelievably I saw that it was a shawl. Aside from missing a crown the fat, white goose wore a shawl like a little king across its back, tied with a simple knot around its neck.

There were items that accidentally became attached to ducks like rings of bread or the plastic loops from beer cans, but a small knitted shawl? For real?!

It looked to the other geese that surrounded it and all noises ceased. They awaited their King's speech.

I had left my bottle on the grass, a dull tingle on my lips made me want what was left within. But as much as I wanted to retrieve it to top up my euphoria, this whole… scenario, if that was the right word, had me captivated. Maybe Grandma had known this about the geese. Maybe their fascinating rituals gave her something to look forward to.

12 Days Of Christmas 2016

It just too weird.

I closed my eyes as a dizzy spell, a big one, rolled through me, I regained my sight to see not only the big goose looking right at me, but the six surrounding the pile also eyeing me.

Should I be scared? The drink was stopping me from reacting that quickly. All I saw was a bunch of noisy ducks finally being quiet as they tilted their heads in my direction.

The shawled goose raised its beak into the air, its long slender neck pointing upwards, and a long low note resonated from its bill like wind through a conch shell.

"He… came. He… came. He… came" A sudden chant filled the crater. I looked about expecting to find out I wasn't alone, a couple of birdwatchers maybe studying the birds or something.

Maybe it was someone's phone nearby? Because there was no way that English chant was coming from the birds that were opening and closing their beaks.

I spun around looking for the source of the chanting, the weirdness of the situation giving me a moment's clarity. The trees surrounding me were spindly, dead and black as though destroyed by fire. Where green should have been, there was only white, the plump white bodies of geese.

Squashed together, lining the thicker low branches, the birds looked down at me.

"He… came. He… came. He… came."

My grandma's words came back to me as visions of the crumpled note in her dead hand replayed.

"Don't forget to feed the geese lad, when I'm gone. Don't forget to feed the geese lad."

Don't let them take the geese.

Don't let them take the geese.

My grandma sitting in front of unwatched television programmes, cackling,

Christmas is coming,

The goose is getting fat,

Please put a penny in the old man's hat.

If you haven't got a penny a ha'penny will do,

If you haven't got that then God bless you.

Their beaks moved in time with the chanting too, and then it stopped.

"She... promised!" the big goose said, I span to look at it. "She… delivered!"

How did it talk like that? Had I been more drunk than I thought?

I didn't waste time contemplating that, I wanted out of there. I spun back around to see the birds on the low branches all flap their wings and swoop towards me. The ones that landed on me began pecking, nipping at me with their beaks. I beat them away with my fists and arms but the insistent pecking began to numb my arms like thousands of pinches.

When they surrounded me and nipped hard enough to break through the numb feeling of my drink I panicked even more.

I flailed my arms, I did my best but was quickly forced to the ground by the sheer number of the feathered monsters.

And… do you want to know something funny? When the one clambered onto my face and began to poke at my eyes, causing me a great amount of pain, as I lay there buried by all its friends, I didn't think about escaping. As my right eye was mashed and squished by the bird's strong, prodding beak, all I could think about as the world began to lose all meaning were my grandma's words.

Don't forget to feed the geese lad, when I'm gone.

Don't forget to feed the geese lad.

Don't forget to feed the geese lad.

12 Days Of Christmas 2016

Don't forget to feed the geese lad.

Don't forget to feed the geese lad.

12 Days Of Christmas 2016

12 Days Of Christmas 2016

Five Gold Rings - Betty Breen

December 25th: 7:45am

DANNY AWOKE WITH THE slam of the front door. He rolled over and in the empty space his wife usually slept in lay a big wrapped box. He sat up and noticed a note on top:

Didn't want to wake you. Here's a little something. Love you always, Mary xxx

A tightness arose in his chest. Mary was such a kind and giving person. Maybe he was making a mistake. Maybe he should give his marriage another go. Opening the drawer to his little bed side cabinet he reached in and turned on his phone.

1 NEW MESSAGE: JUST FOR YOU XX

Attached was a multimedia message. He could see a pair of breasts surrounded by bubbles, the tips of slender fingers gently rested on the left nipple. As quickly as the tightness had invaded his body, it disappeared. Jumping out of bed and into the shower, Danny's excitement was almost tangible. He got himself ready and retrieved the presents he had hidden under the bed. Just as he was about to leave he remembered the box. He ran up the stairs and ripped open the neat wrapping. Inside was a photo of him and his wife on their wedding day. Both smiling at the camera, both looking so happy. He turned it around to read the handwritten note:

'til death do us part x

That's a bit odd, Danny thought before throwing the picture back into the box and making his exit.

It was only a short walk and today he was practically running. The streets were empty, families obviously wrapped up inside opening their gifts. He knew he wouldn't be seen. Arriving just after 9 o'clock he sprang up to the 6th floor of the newly built block of flats. Catching his breath at the top, Danny reached into his pocket for the door key.

'Oh shit,' Danny said. 'Where did I put it?'

Danny started turning out his pockets, sure he had left it in his coat. Not wanting to waste any more time he decided to just knock. He raised the knocker on number 603. The door was already open. She must have heard me coming, he thought.

'Hey sexy, it's me,' Danny called out closing the door behind him. He slipped off his shoes in the tiny hall before moving into the lounge. It was dark, all the lights were off, but there was a flicker from the many candles that had been placed around.

'Hey baby, where are you?'

Still no reply. He walked around the coffee table to the kitchen diner. He saw the dining table which was fully laid for what looked like a family feast. Suddenly, Danny felt something hitting the back of his head. The room went black just before his face hit the floor.

December 15th: 9:30pm

Every year for the past ten Danny did the same thing. He would forget about Christmas, forget his wife loved to be spoilt with jewellery of some kind. He would basically forget to do any shopping until the very last minute. This year however he had set his phone to remind him, daily. Danny had to be in top of it this year. Not only did he have to buy for his wife, but this year he also had to find something for his mistress. Danny wasn't into sleeping around, but when his boss hired Tiffany as his new secretary, he fell head over heels. In lust that is. Pure sexual lust. Tiffany had come onto him first, cornering him in the office supply cupboard. How could he say no to her? She was gorgeous, and she wanted him. The constant ache that had been in Danny's groan since her arrival was enough to tell him he couldn't say no.

That was the first time they had fucked. Seven months and five days earlier. Since then he'd lost count of how many late-night meetings, or office training days he had told his wife he had to attend. Danny wasn't in love with

Tiffany but he wanted to get her something special, purely because he knew how he'd get thanked.

As Danny thought about this, he realised that his pyjamas were rising with his growing excitement.

'Thinking about something are we?'

Danny's wife, Mary, was sitting across the room, both of them occupying their very average living room. Similarly that's how Danny would describe his marriage: boring.

'Uh what?' Danny adjusted himself awkwardly.

'It's okay darling. You know I am your wife,' Mary said with a cheesy wink.

At that Danny left the room. 'I'm going to bed,' he said.

Danny hurried up to the bathroom. Locking the door behind him he reached for his phone and searched through some of the images Tiffany had sent him. After Danny absorbed himself in the memories of how Tiffany tasted, how smooth her skin was to touch, he had a shower. Finishing up he headed to bed.

Mary was already there. Lying on top of the duvet, wearing nothing but her plain beige "granny" pants and non-wired bra. She looked up at him and smiled.

'I thought maybe you might need a hand?'

'Oh, no don't worry. I'm pretty tired actually.'

Forcing out a yawn Danny got into bed, avoiding any eye contact with his wife.

'You sure baby?' Mary ran a hand through his curly black hair.

'Yeah. Maybe tomorrow?' he said.

'Okay Dan-Dan.'

Mary pecked her husband on the cheek before covering herself with a nighty that looked like something out of a Jane Austen movie.

'How's the shopping going?' she asked.

'I'm taking a half day tomorrow,' he said. 'Only one or two bits left.'

'I can't wait for you to see yours.' Mary tensed up. 'The look on your face is going to be priceless.'

Danny had never seen Mary so passionate. In fact, the last few weeks she had started acting strange. She was still the same old Mary who never went against her routine, but she had this excited, child-like attitude. Danny had questioned whether she could be cheating on him, but he had quickly discarded the thought. Mary wasn't the type, she was more of a cosy night in, wearing her big fluffy socks watching shit on the box.

'You remember I have to pop to the office?' Danny said

'Yeah. You can have it after.'

Danny needed to see Tiffany and Mary never seemed to question him about his work, so it was the perfect excuse.

'Anyways. Night.' Danny rolled over and clicked off his light.

December 16th: 8:35am

Danny rushed out the house, avoiding any time with his wife. He was stiff all over after having slept so far on his side of the bed. It took all his concentration not to fall off. He grabbed his breakfast from the small coffee shop opposite the office. As he sipped his double shot Americano his phone buzzed.

2 NEW MESSAGES

He opened the inbox. One was from Mary, the other from Tiffany.

Dreamt about u all night. Cant wait 2 c u sexy. T XXX

12 Days Of Christmas 2016

Danny felt his groan stiffen.

Can u get milk plz. Mary x

When did life get so boring, he thought? Danny downed his drink and threw the cup into the nearby bin. As he climbed the 8 flights of stairs to his office he thought about Mary and their marriage. They had been together so long, ten years, five of which as husband and wife. Thinking back, it had always been boring, it just seemed to have happened. Tiffany was fun, energetic. She made him feel young again, alive and free. Half way up the stairs his phone buzzed again.

Sat in store cupboard all hot and wet. T XOXOXO

Danny started taking the steps two at a time. 'This is the best Christmas yet.'

December 25th: 9:55am

Danny felt groggy. His head was thumping and as he raised it his neck felt stiff. Looking up he could see Tiffany, sitting naked with something stuffed in her mouth. Her eyes were wide and it sounded like she was trying to scream. Danny was sat up at the dining table, Tiffany directly opposite. He tried to rub his head but his wrists were tied to the arms of the chair. He realised he was also naked, and that his ankles were bound.

'What the fuck?' Danny said, his head screaming at him.

'Tiff baby, what the fuck is going on?'

Tiffany, still gagged, wriggled around making unintelligible noises.

December 16th: 12:55pm

Danny got through his morning by remembering his sweet surprise from Tiffany. Danny packed up his brief case and made his way out of the office.

'Yo Dan, mrs on line two,' his boss shouted across to him.

Danny slumped as he picked up the phone on his desk.

'Hey, did you get my message about the milk?' Mary spoke in her posh telephone voice.

'Uh yeah, did I not reply?'

'Well yes, but you didn't mention anything about milk.' Mary sounded cheesy, like she was trying to be coy with him.

'Oh, yeah, sorry. I'll get the milk.'

Danny pulled out his mobile, quickly trying to check his sent box.

'Don't be sorry. Looking forward to seeing you later. I love you.'

'Yeah, you too.' Not really hearing what Mary was saying Danny replaced the receiver and opened his messages. Reading the last one sent to Mary.

Dreamt about u ;) cant wait 2 c u l8r. xxx

'Fuck,' he said aloud, turning a few heads as he rushed out the door. Danny added "PAYG phone" to his shopping list.

With the shopping done, Danny headed home. He had popped to Starbucks first to charge his new phone. Nothing fancy, but it had to have a camera and Wi-Fi. He sent Tiffany a message explaining to text him on this number. As he packed away the lingerie he had bought for his mistress he felt a sudden tightness in his chest. He knew what it was: guilt. He knew what he was doing was wrong, he was having an affair. Cheating on his wife who had done nothing but trust him since day one. But he also felt cheated. Cheated out of having a fun, full adventurous life. If he ended the affair would he then stay faithful forever? Would he ever stop looking for another "Tiffany"? As Danny thought about the answers he slumped back into his chair. He loved Mary but he was bored. Bored of life. Bored of having the same daily routine. He wanted spice, excitement and adventure, isn't that what everyone needed? He loved Mary, but life with her was never going to be any of those things.

On his slow walk home it had started to snow. Danny thought that the gods were mocking him. He was miserable and now he was cold and wet. He decided that after Christmas he was going to end it with Mary. He didn't want Christmas to be tainted for her so after the new-year he'd tell her he was moving out. Of course, he wasn't going to tell her the whole truth. He didn't see the point in being completely honest, otherwise she'd get more than half of their assets.

December 24th: 10:26pm

Danny sat on his armchair drinking a cold beer watching the TV. It was all the usual Christmas shite, but it kept him out of the way. Mary was in the kitchen preparing everything for the next day. He had managed to talk to Tiffany that morning. She told him how lonely her big bed was, hoping Santa would pay her a visit. Danny knew what she wanted. He told her when he'd be around the next day. She had given him a key so that he could just let himself in. That way she could be waiting in her bed.

Mary walked into the lounge stopping Danny's train of thought.

'What time you going out tomorrow?' Mary said.

12 Days Of Christmas 2016

'Around 9.'

'Okay, well I'll pop to mums for around 8.' Mary's mum lived in a nursing home and since her dad died Mary always spent Christmas morning with her. Danny was grateful not to have to go this year. The smell of old people, musty with a heavy stench of urine made his stomach turn.

'Be back by midday?' Mary asked.

'Yup.' Danny slugged back his beer.

December 25th: 10:05am

'What's going on, is you and your dirty little slut here have been caught out.'

Mary was sitting somewhere behind Danny. He tried turning his head to see her but his neck resisted.

'Ah Malteasers, my favourite.' She said.

Danny could hear the crinkling of foil, followed by a loud crunching.

'Mary? What? Please untie me so we can talk,' Danny said still trying to get over his concussion. He looked at Tiffany who looked terrified, the room filled with Mary's munching.

12 Days Of Christmas 2016

'Seriously Mary, what the fuck are you playing at?'

Mary made her way to the dining table. She was dressed in a red knitted Christmas jumper with glittery baubles on the front. Her leggings, clearly a size or more too small, sparkled with the candle light.

'I told you. You and your slut here have been caught out,' Mary said. 'It's funny really isn't it?'

Both Tiffany and Danny failed to see anything amusing about the situation but Mary started to giggle wildly. Throwing her head back like a child.

'Here we all are, it's Christmas day and so far, no one has opened a present.' Mary said through her giggles.

'Look babe, we can talk about this,' Danny thought maybe pleading would help her see how crazy this was. 'Just untie me and we can go, maybe get a coffee? See your mum? Yeah?'

'I'd rather eat. You're hungry aren't you Tiff?'

Tiffany, still gagged, shook her head. Her eyes had filled with tears and as she blinked one dropped down the smooth skin of her cheek.

Danny realised that the table had been perfectly laid, plates with knives and forks, bowls with spoons, and wine glasses, each displaying a carefully swanned napkin. Mary reached forward and lifted the top from what looked like an old-fashioned serving dish. Made from silver with intricate engravings she clutched the handle and raised it over her head with a resounding 'ta-da.'

Tiffany gasped, frantically moving trying to free herself. Danny looked at what was on the dish. Reflecting the twinkling candlelight was a large, wooden handled meat cleaver.

'Woooo, what the fuck? Come on Mary, quit with the games now,' Danny said.

'Games? I like games. Let's play one, shall we?' Mary said, sounding almost psychotic. 'You like playing games Dan-Dan, don't you? For too long you've been playing games with me. I think it's my turn now to choose what we play.'

Mary calmly picked up the cleaver, bringing it up to her face, she smiled like a child on Christmas morning.

'Do you know how many years we've been married Tiff? 5 years,' Mary said, not waiting for an answer. 'That's 5 long years of my life being treated as a fool.'

She slammed the cleaver down into the wooden table.

'So let's celebrate. 5 courses for the 5 years we've been together.'

Mary stood up and collected 5 plates from the side, she placed them down onto the table. The plates were brilliant white, each with a beautiful perfect gold ring around the edge. Danny recognised them straight away. It was their wedding china. He remembered making a joke about them, but that was furthest from his mind.

'You know that's always been my favourite line. "5 golden rings",' Mary sang. 'Just how different it is from the rest. That's why I chose these. Remember Dan-Dan?'

He didn't want to remember. Right now, he just wanted her to shut up.

'I wanted to get married 5 days before Christmas but you wanted a summer wedding. You like getting what you want don't you?' Once again not waiting for an answer Mary pulled the cleaver from the table. 'But I'm waffling. Let's eat!'

With that, Mary brought the instrument down between Tiffany's right ear and scalp. The knife slipped through as if it was slicing through air. Tiffany screamed through her gag as Danny watched the blood pour down her neck. Mary repeated the operation on the other side.

'What the fuck!!' Danny felt sick at the sight of Tiffany's blood flowing down her shoulders, he heard it drip on the wooden flooring. Mary picked up the two ears and placed them on to one of the gold rimmed plates. She hummed, but it didn't drown out Tiffany's sobs.

'Don't worry honey, dinner's on its way. These spoilt brats, so impatient,' Mary said.

'Mary, seriously, stop this, now!' Danny was practically shouting, trying to pull himself free. His bounds were too tight and they were starting to cut into the flesh of his wrists.

'What to do, what to do?' Mary said. 'I know, you loved these didn't you?' Mary grasped one of Tiffany's bare breasts. She started to cut down, hacking through the fatty tissue. The knife once again glided through with ease, Mary seemed to slow down, taking her time.

'Oh would you look at that, they are real!' Mary slopped the fatty piece of meat that once sat perfectly on Tiffany's chest onto a plate. Quickly starting on the next, Danny threw up. The smell of blood and vomit assaulted his nose. Tiffany was silent, but still breathing. Smiling manically, Mary raised the cleaver. Making a grunt she slammed it down. Tiffany's hand fell to the floor with a thud. The whites of her wrist bone visible for a second, then the blood trickled out, dripping freely to the ground. Mary straightened her arms and again slammed down the cleaver, chopping the other hand clean off.

'PLEASE STOP!' Danny pleaded, crying.

'Not 'til we have 5 courses dear.'

Tiffany's head had slumped forward, her chin resting on her flat open chest. Mary grabbed the blood matted hair and pulled out the gag that was wedged in Tiffany's mouth. Danny vomited again, the gag was covered with her thick green bile. Mary picked up a pair of pliers. Letting Tiffany's head fall back, Mary reached inside the open mouth and pulled out the tongue.

'STOP PLEASE.'

When there was no more length to pull out Mary picked up her knife and sliced through the tongue. The limp lifeless muscle hanging from the pliers, splatted onto the fourth plate. Tiffany started retching as blood flowed from her mouth.

'Tiff, Tiff, look at me baby,' Danny said. 'Mary, fucking stop this you psycho bitch.'

Tiffany gurgled and moaned, tears fell mixing with snot and blood. The smell of urine now joined the smell of vomit and metallic blood.

'I'm so sorry baby. It's okay. You're okay.'

'Shush now.' Mary stroked the girl's pale face before running the red stained blade through Tiffany's belly, slicing through the navel. Tiffany's insides spilled from her body. Mary placed the knife down onto the table before grabbing the fallen intestines. Sitting on a dining chair, she pulled the bowels with her. She piled it on to the last plate, slicing off the end when she couldn't fit any more on. Danny looked at the parts of the innocent girl he had madly lusted over.

Mary placed her hands together in prayer and closed her eyes.

'Dear lord, please make us truly thankful for what we are about to receive. Amen.'

12 Days Of Christmas 2016

Four Calling Birds – Jessica McHugh

HE'S FOUR WHISKEYS DEEP when the sea howls like a banshee with a crowning babe. The walls shudder and splinter, and the ocean pours unchecked into the saloon. It screams louder than the rakehells clogging the bar on the bay, but nary a man bats an eye at the din, nor at the devil rising about his boots. Only Philip Cook lifts his feet in fear.

A wave lavishes his barstool with foam, and his throat constricts so tight he can barely breathe. A funny little whistle is all he gets, and he has to growl until the vibration relaxes his gullet enough to fill his lungs.

Men roar with laughter nearby, and Philip's certain it's for him. Lousy with dutch courage, they splash through the saloon like the rising ocean is a miracle, but Philip knows the truth.

The sea is a greater danger than any of them realize, for with its great appetite comes the torment of expulsion. They don't know how badly the sea can chew a man up, or how it can spit him out into a world that expects him to be the same. Mockery rides their bones natural as muscle, a quilt of clove-hitch knots exquisitely layered beneath a tough brown hide Philip once called home. It shields them here, but the waves would loosen them like milk teeth and decorate the shores with the bleached shells of these proud privateers.

The water rises, and the dead man thirsts.

He's frightfully pale these days. He hasn't touched the ocean since the wreck, but patches of ulcerous sea salt coat his skin. Daily, perhaps hourly, the scabrous disease spreads. He hides the scales beneath sleeves and scarves, but the more the ocean encroaches on the saloon, the soggier his secrets become. Pus leaks through his clothing until he's greasy from head to toe and a foul stench rises thick from his bones.

Much though the Baratarians favor their gin and whores, Philip's reek flushes many patrons from the saloon. They cut him infernal on their way out, eyes to their bootlaces but minds aflutter with ridicule. The ones who stay in the bar are no shock to Philip, for he has fallen into their ill-fated crew. Upon this, his fifth year trapped in the bay, he has learned well to detect such wraiths and promptly forget them.

Save one. Save today.

The woman is an umber heap of flesh with hair like a molting crow. She's been here forever, they say, but no one in Barataria Bay spins the same yarn about the crone. She wears gossip like the pelt of a black bear, piled high and doubling her mass as she cobwebs the corner of the saloon. The bag at her side is also a fixture of the bar, but unlike the woman, no one disputes its contents. The bag is an organ of Chaos, neither good nor evil but frolicsome as the sea. It produces both curse and charm, and what the organ consumes Philip can only guess, but after half a decade of boasts from sailors seeking the crow woman's help, desperation has sacked his many suspicions.

He breathes through the suffocating fear, and the swelling waves spit acidic water in retaliation, but he grips the chair harder. Bracing himself for the devil's bite, he lowers one foot to the floor, but he finds the boards thankfully dry. The ocean retreats from his tattered boots, opening a path to the crow woman. It is first fair weather he's encountered since he tried to flee notorious Lafittes in the Henrietta.

The crone doesn't lift her head when he approaches but acknowledges him with a bitter whisper: "You shoulda gone down with her."

All around him the tavern teems with sharks and shrapnel and the bellowing locker song. It keens ravenous through his veins and sloshes in his skull so violent his brain is moldy bread in bilgewater.

"What'd you say to me?" he asks her.

The woman's feathers dance like ebony flame as she clears her throat. "I say you best got money, son."

The hungry waves quiet, and Philip nods. "Aye, I've got money."

The crow woman lifts her head slowly as if assembling each layer of her human costume like a puzzle on a turning screw. Her hair falls back from her face, a ragged raven trim for her sloppy, tiered physique and the white-blue eyes half-sunk in her skin. They do not gleam when fixed upon Philip. They are dead, discarded things, like gems scratched to hell in the crevice of a ditty box. When Philip recoils, her smirk puckers to an aphid-laden rose. "Blood money is it?"

He grits his teeth. There's no point denying his sins anymore. The plucky son of a mariner priest who never turned a card nor ran afoul his fellow man is naught but a scoundrel now, a fool who paid dearly for his first risk with the Henrietta and her crew.

He's still drowning after all these years, just in a different sea. And he still prays for a good death—a sailor's death.

He put a stopper in that dream long ago, he assumes. Pieces of him survived the wreck, true, but his rigging's a mess. Splintered masts and knotted cordage can't catch a fine wind, and as the water churns around him, he knows prayers are wasted time he could spend drinking. Philip is a good man no more, nor a man of the sea. For his treachery, God cast him from paradise and into the devilish deep, but so foulsome was Philip's flavor, even the bitter sea would not digest him.

What is a man rejected by both Heaven and Hell? No man at all, he reckons. The Barataria whores treat him with less regard than the horned lizards, and the only work suited to him now is best done by a mad dog.

"Aye," speaks the mongrel. "Blood money it is."

The witch waves a finger in the air, her grin webbed in ungoliant dark. Two whiskeys deliver themselves, and Philip falls into both. The woman never drinks, and he suspects why. She's fattening him up, dulling his wits, and he doesn't give a fig. Logic didn't stop him from joining the Lafittes' high-stakes poker game. It didn't stop him betting goods he didn't have or he lost to the Lafittes, and it won't stop him now.

"You wish to know the sea again," she says, and Philip gulps hard, losing droplets of precious oil down his chin.

He sucks the lint-liquor from his tunic and shakes his head. "I've known it well, and it has known me," he says, licking his lips. Gaze rolling around the saloon, he catches the muddy glint of his fellow wraiths. "I wish to start afresh, but when I think of sailing, I—I—" Philip's lungs parch to a salt cave of toxic air. He grips the tabletop, and his face drains to a sickly green as the furniture pitches and spins. With a grunt, he wrangles the table to stillness, and his bellows expand with fresh oxygen. After a few moments of steadying breath, he says, "Surviving that wreck ruined everything I prized about myself. I've done my time, repaid my debts to the Lafittes. I don't want to be afraid anymore. I want the sea to recognize me. I want to be unknown."

"No sins to lug around or repent. How noble."

He slams his fist on the table, juddering the glasses but not the woman. "I made a mistake!"

The crow woman gestures for more whiskey, and Philip Cook sits opposite with his claws open in wait. The waves close around them, and though Philip's moldering stench rises like hot swamp gas, she does not recoil like the others. The soggier he is, the further across the table she oozes.

"Can you help me or not?" he asks.

"We shall see," she says and propels the drink to his palm. "First, tell me how you died."

He remembers every second of that fateful day. They run through him like wild horses in the time between his hand closing on the glass and liquor raining divine fire in his gut. Her request is an auger hollowing the parts of him that harbor the good of his past—his ambitions, his faith, his father's warnings. Philip hangs his head, and the whiskey makes a lantern of him, hotheaded and incapable of anything but plateau and death.

"It was my first delivery to the Americas," he says. "My father, a former sailor turned priest, had long warned me of the place. I took his yarns as pure fancy back then, so queer were the tales he spun of low-moral mariners. Save a few, I found most seamen lacking our Christian values, but he spoke of these men like he spoke of demons. America, he said, was all at sea—a land too dotty to know it would sink under the weight of its bacchanalia."

"But you went anyway."

He nods. "I got a job in Van Dieman's Land on the Henrietta, a packet bound for the Gulf of Mexico. Whatever awaited me in America, the pay was worth the risk."

"And the adventure, I reckon," the woman says. "Come now, was your father wrong about this world?"

"No. He was wrong about me," says Philip Cook. "He thought I was strong, and I believed him, but I fell easy into the game. When my soul was at stake, I lost all and fled." He clenches his jaw, but a deadly cold deluge surges down his throat. He smacks his chest as he sputters up salt crystals and gasps for air.

His whiskey glass is full again, and he gulps deep to melt the salt. When his chest is aflame with delicious liquor-breath, he frowns and taps the lip of the cup.

"Naivety was the blaze that blew the sticks out of the Henrietta," he says. "The Lafittes lit the cannons, but it was my fault she sank. It was my fault the crew went with her."

"All but you."

"More's the pity. I wished to remain with that sacred crew, the most revered of God's children. Like Noah, a jolly survivor of the flood," he says. "I wanted to die like that more than anything in my natural, swallowed by the godly sea."

"Ah, but naivety sinks you still," she says. "The sea is not godly, boy. Under the clouded crests and emerald swells, beneath the beauty of its skins and scales, the sea is the devil's most luxurious costume. You have lost sight of that, like a snake charmer who makes a deadly pet of his serpent. One can respect the devil, but you must fear him as well. The same goes for God, if you want the truth of it." Her nose lifts, and her opal eyes glitter at the ceiling. "I fear it will take more than money to save you, boy. You are marked to the bone. However..."

The crow woman licks her lips, which turn pale and slimy as dead salmon. She pulls the chaos bag into her lap and with a greasy sneer, removes a squishy object. "This," she says, unwrapping the damp cloth, "will strip your fear of the sea and protect you from its ire."

12 Days Of Christmas 2016

The thing looks like congealed milk tangled in an ivory fishing net, colorless but reeking as if hued by shit and murder. Philip hovers his fingers over the creamy cobweb, and the roiling waves shrink to timid whitecaps.

"A caul..." The voice doesn't feel like his when it claws its way up his throat, but the ocean in the saloon retreats further, so Philip embraces the new rasp to bellow. "It's a caul!"

The woman wrinkles her nose in amusement. "Indeed. Chaos must favor you. A caul is a powerful weapon. Those born with this membrane as a helm are said to be blessed, even magical. But this baby..." She raises her hands until Philip fingers rest gently on the weeping meat. "...was born en caul, completely within her amniotic sac. They say things about children like that, too."

It's warm against his fingertips, and though its putrid scent has not freshened, he's used to it now, even glad of it.

"They breathe water," Philip says. "A baby born en caul can never drown." He snatches for it, but the crow woman's hand disappears into the darkness of her chaos bag, and her face stretches with a gnarled rictus.

"About my payment."

"I thought you didn't want my money."

"I don't. But it ain't me doing the wanting. There's a balance to such things, you see, and this here talisman requires something big in trade. It'll be dangerous, I reckon, but you strike me as a man chapped enough to sense the good in the risk. Just once more."

The voice comes again, ritualistic as erosion as it scrapes over his tongue. He recognizes it at last, and his eyes fill with water. "Once more, and I can go home?"

"Bring me what chaos demands, and your home can sway with the sea, as near or as far from Barataria as you wish." She puckers her pale lips with a sloppy squelch and adds, "...Sailor."

Philip swears he hears men laughing from the quay. As he extends his hand to the crow woman, he vows those men will not laugh long. He doesn't recall speaking, but she shakes his hand and says, "Well done you."

Some people say the sea is hungry or lonely—that's why it takes so many good men—but it's not about consumption or company with that devil. It's not even a warning to the men who dare to sail. It's a message to the god who dares to make sailors of men.

Philip Cook knows that now, and with the crow woman's help, he can win back his dominion over the sea. It does not fear much, granted, but there is terror in its inexorable depths. It does not fear the sailor, rather the one who keeps him afloat: a ship, an indomitable woman who coasts the devil's throat, around every fang, and breaks herself to bits to save the one she loves.

His was Henrietta. She's gone now, but there are plenty to take her place. Constance, Virginia, Iris... When he is cured of his fear, he will board the next great lady and go.

Phillip draws several eyes as he limps from the saloon. It's no shock. He's barely shuffled a mile a year for the last five and never toward the sea, but there hasn't been day the water hasn't stalked him. He's defended each flood and trickle to the people of Barataria Bay, sometimes to skull-thumpings he hoped might free him, but now that Philip stands upon the beach, his tattered shoes sinking into its solicitous tissue, he knows how broken he's been without it.

The haunting waves were phantoms all. The daily drownings, the mockery, his rancid leprous skin—are nothing compared to the devil itself. Its ravenous screams are lovelier up close, but the nearer he trudges, the daring his disease becomes. The salty scales extend down the backs of his hands, hardening his joints.

"You are long dead," the crow woman told him. "You pretend you're like the others, the sailors, someone your father could love, but you are a monster, Philip Cook. You need to die again. You need to die better."

"How?"

He stands a meter from the sea's last foamy kiss, his face downturned and the witch's voice resounding in his mind.

"Four identical pearls," said the witch, "black as the loveliest night and more precious than God's own cunt. With a power like that, chaos will deliver the cure you seek. You may take the caul and, fearless, reintroduce yourself to the sea, but first you must pay."

The beach is speckled with black stones, black seaweed, black freckles of marine flesh, but nothing to fit so lofty a description. His search is cut short anyway once the water gets a taste.

Waves storm his feet with seaweed lassos that drag him to the ground. The sand and shells dig at his skin, but his disease protects him like a virgin ship. Salt and stench weave a net of scars that armor his flesh, but boggy surf rushes down his throat like it's making up for lost time. It both devours and cocoons, shocking him with wallops of oxygen between acrid gluts. He's not sure what to expect when he opens his eyes beneath the waves, but he assumed hellish sights over the heavenly light that radiates from the ocean floor. Deep in the atlantic green, brighter than a Christmas moon, a primordial glow calls Philip Cook down into a familiar oblivion. There, he is as useless as Henrietta's boards, as good as his father's prayers a world away, but the brilliant, black-lipped oyster below him has other plans.

12 Days Of Christmas 2016

The gargantuan oyster would be out of place even in its native Tahiti. Portions of its prehistoric girth are still buried in the silt—he'll have to excavate it to open it—but he knows at first touch that this buried treasure can brighten a dead man.

In clawing sand from the shell, Philip uncovers the source of its light. Hashes in the oyster's bulbous shell pulse in shanty rhythms that resurrect all the years he spent working his father's ship, before the sea sent the mariner scurrying to hide under the church's skirt. The song's rhythms make certain promises, and the light makes proposals he wouldn't dare refuse.

His fingers curl under the oyster's lip, but his heart is already inside. The hashes of lights flicker, and the shanty ceases, but when Philip finally pries the oyster open, four large onyx pearls emit a glow immaculate and complex as a vascular map. Congruent with their elusive magic, the pearls are slippery as live eels. Holding two at a time is rotten work, four is impossible, and the oyster is too large to lug to the surface.

Philip has no other choice. He must hoist the treasures in a different cradle.

One by one, the ex-sailor shoves the pearls into his mouth, locks them behind his teeth, and swallows their light. Despite their size, the pearls go down easy as ice cubes and rumsweat, but with the last jewel consumed, so go the sea's enchantments. A shift in oceanic pressure squeezes remnant air from Philip's body, and it bubbles out of his pores with a sickening pop. Salt invades his eyeballs and crystallizes his blood vessels, but the stone quartet in his belly expand like bubbles that lift him from the empty mollusk.

He bursts from the surface and careless waves cast him to the freckled shore. He's weak as blanched straw and gasping for air when he lands, but in the moments between flashes of heaven and death-light, he feels alive for the first time in years. But when Philip stands safe on the shore, he realizes he doesn't need the safety as he once did. With a jubilant yawp, he runs back to the water. He kicks it. He stomps through it and cackles like the men in the saloon as he teases the angry surf. The only thing that can stop him now is the sudden roar of pain in his gut.

His hands jump to his belly like an expectant mother, and he smiles. The pearls. This is their doing. The pearls have restored his dash-fire. The pearls have stripped his name from the devil's tongue and cured him. Why then, he wonders, should he go back for the caul?

The shanty song begins anew. The locker song thumps jolly from the devil's heart, and somewhere upon its flesh, men work to keep the fiend at bay. He longs to be with them, and now he can be. He'll bargain his way into a new woman's life. He'll befriend her, tend her, and the treasures in his stomach will send him home.

But what if the pearls' enchantments are only temporary? What if when he dries out or passes the gems, they prove to be a poor substitute for the caul's power?

Gritting his teeth, Philip scans the beach. The freckles in the sand could be worthless coal or rock or chunks of excrement polished by the waves, but they shine with extraordinary potential now. They, too, can be precious.

Philip enters the saloon, and the crow woman lifts a threadbare eyebrow as if detecting his briny tang. A dirty smile spreads her face, and she unfolds her hands. Her palms resemble the bottom of a Staffy Bull's paws, all fat pads and gnarled scars from a lifetime of dogfighting. The beach rubbish Philip sanded and shaped might not be perfect pearls, but it doesn't appear her sense of touch is any better than her sight.

He drops them onto her bloated palm, and the rocks ride the valleys between her scarred hills of flesh. With a satisfied grin, she reaches into her bag, deeper than its cloth bottom, and releases the porky pearls to chaos. Following a few winges and squeals, she withdraws her hand, this time holding the damp caul as promised.

"I reckon our deal is ended," says the crone. "What will do you now?"

Philip tucks the caul into his ditty bag and smirks. "I'm leaving this godforsaken island before it sinks under the weight of its bacchanalia."

"Pity. I so enjoy a redemption story, and I didn't think yours was ended just yet."

He draws close to her. It's the first time he's ventured far enough past his own stench to catch a whiff of hers, and he's shocked to find her sweetly perfumed. This woman with frayed plumage all about her large brown face smells rich and buttery. She smells of the open air. She smells of sugar and tobacco. She smells of desert lime.

"You're always here," he says suspiciously. "Every day."

"True."

"But you smell like the outside world. You smell like my home."

"Funny."

"But you're always here."

"You said that."

He sniffs again. There's something sweeter than lime. Something dry and cloying as the smell of his father's church.

Eyes narrowed, he growls. "What the hell are you anyway?"

She closes her eyes and inhales deeply. "That's a question best asked before our deal, don't you think? What matters now is who you are. Sad as it is, I suspected it might end this way, so I've secured you passage from the gulf. The Kermit Line's Virginia sails on the hour, and they're expecting you."

Philip Cook is a new man. The caul is the most dependable sail, and the black pearls are mermaids in his belly. They dance and drag his organs to death but remain the most glorious creatures in creation, flirting with the underside of his skin.

The quay rollicks with departures. He strolls the docks dripping with prospect, but he's never felt drier or more divine. If the crow woman's bag is an organ of chaos, Philip Cook is an organ of the sun itself, a scorched seed that tames the tides and cheers the mad star's apathy toward men.

The sailors who laughed at Philip for five years titter and blush like Easter children at his approach, and why shouldn't they? Every step to the sea bakes his pale skin until the day's colors belong to him. He is both ship and champagne to these brutes, and he will break majestic upon the virgin waves. All those years he spent waterlogged and dreaming, he imagined could be gallant and strong like he was on the Henrietta. He isn't dotty enough to think he's back to being that spry young thing, but a new splendor possesses him. What light danced in the sea now dances in Philip, blasting away the crusted salt and grime to reveal the sailor in wait. This, four pieces of immortality explain, is the closest a man comes to divinity. His peak years were the cost—family and pride too—but it's worth it to be something beyond mortal. He has no fear of the devil again. He is a sailor again.

The Red Star Packet Line isn't doing well these days. Sailing under the blue flag of Robert Kermit, the Virginia is smaller than the ships of the line's red and white heyday, but Philip's grateful to any seaworthy woman willing to carry him away.

She and her saintly crew are more than willing. Captain E.C. Nickels and his men greet Philip as a long-lost brother as he boards the ship. They shake his hand and embrace him. They ask him about his standard shifts, if he'd be willing to take the crow's nest, and he plows merrily through the landlubber rust. He's deep in discussion about his berth when he notices a dewy sailor wink at the captain and tosses the gangplank aside.

A palpable unease draws the light from Cook's bones. The pearls cool in his belly, itchy as icy feathers from the crow woman's scalp as a sailor leans over his shoulder with a curtain of foamy saliva gathered between his chapped lips. "You spoke to the witch, yeah? What'd she say? What'd she give?"

"I don't get your meaning, mate."

Captain Nickels shoves his sneer in Philip's face. "You been a sandcrab for five years, and now you're fit as a fiddle? I don't buy it. You're changed. That's what the lady does."

"God changed me. He's finally forgiven me my sins."

"God serves the lady, poor devil. Your sins are her salvation."

The Virginia crew latches onto their long-lost brother and drags him fore, ransacking his pockets as they slam him against the rail. Captain Nickels hoots when he finds the wad of cloth in Cook's coat, but his face goes gray when the woman with a molted coif toddles across the deck.

The crone's alabaster eyes roll sluggish in her porridge face, but her smile bubbles up with cruel precision. "Hello, sailor."

The pillage in his belly twists with each syllable, accentuating the roar in his voice. "What is this?" Philip demands. "We had a deal!"

"Aye, we did, and you fulfilled your part as shoddily as expected," says the crow woman. "This arrangement could've been clean, but you got greedy as the sea. One whiff of a future you thought lost, and you went off your chump, thieving like you done every day since the wreck."

Tears fill Cook's eyes, and regret pours down his cheeks like scalding oil.

He swallows hard, and the rocks in his belly clatter like liar's dice. "Once more," he whispers. "I thought it worth the risk, just once more."

The crow woman nods to the sailor and says, "We shall see."

Their fingers sink into Philip's spongy flesh and wring out every drop of bravery. It takes no effort at all, which leads him to believe the hope and magic the woman gave him was mere fancy, but when the men hurl him overboard, when water floods his bellows and the depths go to work strangling his guts, relief washes over the unsatisfactory son of a mariner priest.

Philip doesn't try to swim. He doesn't search his anatomy for pockets of air. And when the last sunbeam flees his body, he does not lament the darkness. His scabs wither and snap free, floating to the surface with the rest of his useless things. He is soft and disgraced and damned—the devil's favorite flavors.

12 Days Of Christmas 2016

Somewhere between life and death, it is dogwatch in Philip Cook's flesh. Everything in him slumbers but four beasts that wrestle in existence, stretching and shredding his body from the inside out. There is little pain while the ebony fledglings quit their pearls and split Philip's guts, but as they wriggle from their broken shells, the clouds of blood and meat thicken. He's living chum, too weak to fight or free the birds tangled in his guts. They don't need his help anyway. Flapping their wings, they pull Philip upward, his veins and tendons knotted in their talons as they rip him from the ocean like balloons of blood and down.

The sailors are gray and retching when the crows lower Phillip onto the deck of the Virginia. They rush to escape, but the witch has already cast the ship into the sea. The crew is trapped in the devil's throat, fated to watch the black pearl birds rip Philip apart. Any moment now, death will come. He closes his eyes and waits. But with the sting of a purring breeze, he detects his wounds are drying. Even his breath seems stronger by the second.

Lifting his head, Philip beholds the birds still tangled in his organs but no longer trying to pull free. They're retreating back inside, reassembling and sewing his body back together as they burrow home, into their ebony eggs. His abdomen is unblemished when he sits up, his touch oddly maternal when his hand falls to his belly. Standing, he recoils at the woman's sly grin and the way the chaos bag shivers with seeming delight.

"What the deuce is this sorcery?" Captain Nickels demands. "You promised us the caul in exchange for this filthy paper jack, witch!"

"That was before I knew Mr. Cook and I still had business," she says.

Philip bares his teeth, and spittle leaps from his trembling lips. "Our deals are done, woman. If ever I see again, it will be too soon."

"Enough of this," says Captain Nickels. He pulls a pistol on the crow woman and sneers. "If you can't honor our bargain, I'll claim my due without honor as well."

The woman's braying is loud to start, but it becomes near deafening when her forehead cracks wide and murder spills from her opal eyes. Crows split the rest of her skull open and fly from her face like a melon spitting its own seeds. They dive at the captain, pecking and tearing his lips and flesh until absent honor is the least of his problems.

Philip's innards writhe and shoot queasy darts down his legs until he collapses to the deck. He tries to hold the devils inside, but the brood's calls are too urgent, and his flesh is butter to their hungry beaks. The fledglings burst again from their sanctuary, dripping with viscera as they go to work on the rest of the Kermit Line crew. Laughter still resounds from the woman's ruptured skull, and her tongue wags mad over a ridge of broken teeth while Philip piles up his soggy pieces.

When the job is done, the birds return to their nests, not a joint or vein misplaced. Philip can feel their every flutter, even as the sea rocks them gently to sleep. He doesn't understand them, but he never understood his kidneys or brain either and thinks them magical. He has a similar invisible tenderness to the birds.

He tries not to show it, but there are no deceptions between he and crow woman now. There are no awkward pauses or judgements. Once the last of the crew is dead, she hardly speaks and dallies less than a minute among the dead. He knows why as readily as now he knows death as a wet dream. She has ports to visit and people to meet. There are pleasures to be had acquiring all the world's perfume. But she leaves, her eyes gleam like iridescent milk, she reaches into the chaos bag, and she removes one last gift.

The satchel is identical to hers, humble and devastating, and it feels like a cannonball when she hangs it from his shoulder. She gives him no instruction. He needs none. But he still thinks this woman, this unsinkable ship, will share something lovely with him on the open sea, even her dirty rotten smile. The smirk starts with bunching umber flesh, but it falls abruptly. The woman's nose sinks into her skull, her teeth loosen and tumble out like overcooked corn, and crows explode out of her brittle cheeks. The flock yanks her up the sky, their talons tangled in muscle and hair, into the screaming divine until the sun burns them away.

He is alone on a ghost ship, a bloody new shade of blessed. He can't keep the Virginia afloat for long, thank God, and when this indomitable woman can sail no more, he will go down with her. Then, fearless and unknown, a dead man will rise again and spread his fledgling wings.

Three French Hens - Mark Leney And Forbes King

"ARE YOU SURE THAT this is the right entrance for the party?" Berenice Brique asked with a note of uncertainty as she followed her two friends down into the dark and forbidden depths of the Catacombs that ran all the way under the city of Paris.

Shawntel Paille led the way with the group's only torch.

"This is the entrance that Pierre told me to use." She assured her friend as she shone the powerful beam into the darkness ahead of her.

The final member of the group was Patience De Bois and she laid her exquisitely manicured hand upon Shawntel's shoulder as much to reassure herself in the encroaching blackness than anything else.

Lewd and puerile graffiti adorned the crumbling walls either side of them and this evidence that other's had been down here before them served somewhat to calm any fears that the girl's may have had.

"This party had better be worth it!" Patience whined as they descended deeper and deeper into the bowels of the Catacombs. "I don't want to end up lost down here and miss Christmas dinner with maman and papa tomorrow."

"If you stick with me we won't get lost, I promise!" Shawntel reiterated with as much patience as she could muster.

It was then that they came to a T-junction in the path that they were following.

"Now which way?" Berenice wondered. "Did Pierre tell you that?"

"No, he didn't!" Shawntel conceded, "But look!"

She shone the torch beam onto the wall ahead of them and there was an arrow that had been spray painted onto the brickwork in a rather disconcerting blood red. It was pointing towards the right.

"We go this way!"

"Are you sure?" Berenice asked.

"Why else would that arrow be there?" Shawntel argued.

"Makes sense to me." Patience shrugged.

Out voted Berenice followed her friends into the right hand passage. The air was cold as their footsteps echoed in the chamber of stone. It occurred to Berenice that this was very much like the castles that her uncle Claude used to tell her about when she was little. In those there were stories of romance, adventure and escapism. These catacombs had none of that feeling. It was dark and cold and she was beginning to feel like this was a very bad idea. She knew little of the catacombs as the stories of ghosts and ghouls didn't interest her. Berenice was a girl who believed in real things, who believed in herself and what she could do. Her papa often said she was as stubborn as stone when she put her mind to it.

"My feet are killing me!" Patience whined in a high pitched voice. She had no tolerance for persistence.

"Stop that." snapped Shawntel. "We don't know what's down here." She looked around the dark nervously. Her sense of scepticism being tested.

Shawntel laughed. "You both should shut up and think about Jean Clyde."

"Jean Clyde?" Patience replied. "Are you serious?"

"I am always serious on the matter of men."

Both Shawntel and Patience sighed. Jean Clyde was only the city's most eligible bachelor. He was strapping and blonde with a face carved by the gods themselves. Both girls wondered if his business down below was carved from the gods too. Berenice thought he was the only reason that Shawntel was making this trip at all. According to Shawntel, the best things in life always involved men. She was a very attractive girl, medium height, brown hair falling to the shoulders, big breasts and a slim waistline. Now that Berenice knew that Jean Clyde was going to be here, she knew what Shawntel planned on doing. Jean Clyde was nothing more than a conquest to her friend, so she could gloat that she'd spread her legs for the bachelor of the city, the man that every girl wanted and she, Shawntel had caught and bedded him.

Berenice had more radical goals than simply enjoying her womanhood. She was an aspiring writer. Her current story was about two romantic dragons trying to survive in a world that was pitted against them. Her last story 'The Case of the Fish' had sold to publishers for good money and allowed her some freedom and the ability to write more, but it was a week by week thing at the moment. It was strange that she had no belief in what she couldn't see, yet Berenice wrote stories on fantasy. Her father remarked often that 'she was unique to the point of absolution'. Her papa just didn't understand. Most people didn't.

They reached an intersection where there were three paths to choose from. They were all dark and all looked as promising as the last.

"Well?" Patience asked.

"I don't know, okay?" snapped Shawntel. "I thought Pierre would be here to guide us. He let us down."

"You mean, you." Berenice corrected. Pierre was your little boy, a pining little thing that had the biggest crush on you."

In the glow of the torchlight, Shawntel gave Berenice a withering look, one that said there would be payback for that slight. Yet, none of this helped them come to a decision.

"Which way are we going? Berenice asked. Her motivation for this party was disappearing by the second. She was beginning to wish that she had stayed at home and continued on her story with a nice glass of pinot. But Patience had talked her into it. She had a skill of doing that. But Berenice let her if she was honest with herself. She spent too much time inside her flat, inside her room. There was a world to explore, she kept telling herself and needed to do so while she was still able to do so.

"Let Shawntel decide." Patience said sweetly. "She wanted us to go to this party, so she should tell us which way to go."

But she doesn't know, thought Berenice. She's as lost as the rest of us. But that won't stop her. Shawntel was like a wolf when cornered. She came out fighting, claws ready for battle. Berenice could already see it in her eyes, a steely determination that she wouldn't be humiliated or embarrassed. Berenice felt sorry for Pierre. He was going to get an ear full from Shawntel at the next available moment. It won't be tonight, but at some point, it was going to happen. Shawntel never let anyone humiliate her like this, especially someone like Pierre.

"Let's try this way." Shawntel pointed the flashlight towards the centre tunnel up ahead.

"Why that one?" Patience asked. "It looks the same as the others?"

"Why not?" Was the only answer that Shawntel would give as she led them into the tunnel.

Berenice had lost all interest in this place, it was dark, spooky and they had no idea where they were going. The only positive at this point, they weren't lost… Yet. She couldn't turn back. Maybe she would talk Patience into returning to the entrance with her, but Shawntel would never turn back, not until she had come to the conclusion on her own that this party doesn't exist, or they couldn't find it. Berenice could never leave Shawntel to wander down here on her own. So, after much reluctance, she followed her two friends further into this stone labyrinth.

They walked further into the darkness, further into the cold stone that was the catacombs of Paris.

"Do you realise that there are over six million dead down here?" Patience asked.

"Nobody needs to know that and who cares?" Shawntel called back over her shoulder. The growing anger in her voice was evident to all.

"I suppose no one does care." Patience replied. "But I thought it was interesting."

"The only thing I'm interested in is this damned party."

None of them were really in the mood for this anymore. It was time for Berenice to end this and put a stop to this pointless journey. "Look, Shawntel, this isn't working. We've spent a good half hour looking for this place, Pierre isn't answering your calls, let's just go."

"Go?" Shawntel whirled around, shadows dancing across her face. "You want to leave and take that whimpering pussycat with you?" She pointed to Patience.

"Hey!"

"I know you're angry, but don't take it out on Patience. She isn't the one that's at fault here."

"Oh, so it's me, is it?" Shawntel asked, her anger rising, like boiling water in a broth. "I offered to give you a night off from your fantasy about, um, what is it? Ah, yes, two dragons in love!"

Berenice folded her arms. "We're going. Stay if you want with all the dead here, but we're going. This farce has been going on long enough." She grabbed Patience's hand and led her back down the tunnel towards the intersection.

"Are we really leaving her? She does have the only torch!"

"No. She will come once she's calmed down." Berenice said, but in her mind she hoped that was the case. Shawntel could be very, very stubborn and right now she was very angry and humiliated. She didn't look behind her, back to Shawntel. She guessed that her friend would be storming off to find this party, just to prove them wrong.

"What? What is that?" Shawntel cried out.

Berenice turned around and saw her friend running towards them. She saw something follow. It looked unreal. Patience wrenched free and ran away.

"What is that?" Berenice asked as she backed away, in revulsion.

"I don't know and I don't want to know." Shawntel grabbed the front of Berenice's blouse so hard she ripped it partly open. "I'm sorry, you were right, I was wrong, let's get out of here!"

The shambling creature coming towards them was no costumed party goer. If it was, then this person would win an award for sure. It was hard to make out in the flashlight, but it looked like a corpse, a man wearing a revolution-style jacket with a grimy shirt. The head was mostly skeletal with pieces of skin and flesh here and there.

"What is that?" Berenice cried out. "That's not possible, you're not possible!"

Shawntel slapped her. "ARE YOU NOT HEARING ME? IT'S TIME TO GO. NOW!" She screamed and pushed her backwards. She fell to the ground. Shawntel sighed and grabbed Berenice's shoulder, hauling her to her feet. "Move, move!"

Berenice took off her heels and threw them at the creature, which didn't slow it down at all. Patience had slipped from her heels and was now running. Berenice could feel the slap of her bare feet against the grainy, cold ground and the rippling of her half opened shirt. Shawntel was wearing a black sleeveless dress. She always looked elegant no matter what she was wearing. Up ahead, Patience was waiting for them. Her courage had returned. "Hurry up, hurry up!"

They reached the intersection. Both Berenice and Shawntel were panting.

"What do we do?" Patience asked.

"We get out of here." Shawntel replied. "Which way did we come in?"

"I don't know!" Patience yelled. "I thought you knew this place!"

"Of course I don't!" Shawntel yelled back. "Do you think I wake up in the morning and think to myself, oh, you know what? I'll go to the bloody catacombs and hang out with six bloody million corpses!"

"Shut up!" Berenice cried. "This isn't..."

A skeletal hand reached from around the corner and grabbed at Shawntel by her black dress and pulled her back into the darkness.

"Shawntel!" Berenice cried out. "We've got to go back for her!"

"Are you crazy?" Patience yelled at her. "What can we do for her? That thing will get us too if we go back now!" She grabbed Berenice's hand and started to pull her away.

Shawntel's screams could be heard around the corner. There was a wet tearing noise like a dog biting into a bloody steak and the beam of Shawntel's fallen torch picked out the droplets of crimson that splashed the illuminated brick work. Shawntel's screams stopped.

Berenice dug in her heels briefly so that she could retrieve Shawntel's torch before allowing Patience to pull her away, hot tears coursing down her cheeks and splashing her blouse.

They continued running along the pitch black tunnel until they came to another fork.

"Which way?" Patience wondered with mounting hysteria.

The laboured, shuffling of the thing could be heard scraping ever closer behind them.

"Shine the torch this way so we can see where we're going!" Patience shouted at Berenice.

Berenice's hands were shaking as she brought the torch around shining it first down into the left hand passageway. The slender pin-prick of light barely penetrated the gloom.

The scraping steps behind them were drawing nearer by the second, accompanied by the sound of wet mucous-filled rasping from the thing's ravaged throat. Also the rancid stench of its decaying flesh was swept along by the cool subterranean breeze, filling Berenice's nostrils and making her want to puke.

Patience screamed as an emaciated cadaver lurched out of the darkness of the right hand passage and clawed at her with broken fingernails. This one had been female once, wearing the tattered remnants of an 18th Century peasant woman's dress. Wispy cobwebs of wizened hair still clung to her peeling scalp and one side of her dress had torn enough to expose a shrivelled breast ending in a blackened nipple, weeping pus like rancid baby's milk.

The jagged nails drew oozing red lines of blood down Patience's bared shoulder, but fortunately the young girl was able to pull away before the creature could get a proper hold of her.

This time it was Berenice's turn to tug Patience away from the impending danger.

"Left it is!" she remarked as they tore off down the passageway.

As they ran Patience noticed a narrow niche in the right side of one wall that looked just wide enough for a person to squeeze into. She twisted out of Berenice's grip and started trying to slide herself into the tight gap.

Berenice stopped running and turned back to look at what her friend was up to.

"Patience, come on!" she cried. "We've got to run!"

"Come with me!" Patience insisted as she struggled further into the niche. "If we go down here they won't find us, or at least they won't be able to follow us!"

"Don't be stupid!" Berenice protested. "We won't fit down there!"

"You won't fit, you mean!" Patience threw back spitefully. "I've gone down two dress sizes this year!" She would have said more, but her eyes widened with panic as she realised that she actually could not get any further into the gap.

Patience started to try and pull herself out of the little alcove and started to sob hysterically when she couldn't come out. She was stuck!

"Help me!" she begged Berenice.

Berenice started forward, her hand outstretched towards Patience's.

The desiccated remains of the shambling undead peasant woman melted from the shadows, her own bony limb extended in a macabre mirror-image of Berenice's gesture, only her intent was to kill, not to save.

Berenice took an involuntary step backwards and this hesitation was all that the dead peasant woman needed.

With one final faltering step her outstretched fingers closed around Patience's throat and the ragged, broken nails ripped through the flesh of the young girl's neck. Patience couldn't even scream as her windpipe was torn open along with vital arteries which ejaculated blood in an explosion of scarlet that painted the right side of the revenant's face and upper body, making the creature look as if it were wearing a grotesque crimson half-mask.

A few of the droplets spattered Berenice's face and blouse and the girl screamed. She shook her head; her whole body was trembling from the shock and trauma of what she had just witnessed. Berenice had lost two of her closest friends and now she was stuck down here alone with two undead supernatural killers. There was no way that she would find her way out of this fucking maze. Would it not be better to end it now? Just stand there and let those things take her?

Even as these thoughts occurred to her she continued to shake her head, but this time in defiance rather than denial. No, she wasn't going to die like that.

The peasant woman was already creeping towards her and now she had been joined by the first cadaverous ghoul that they'd encountered.

Berenice shouted at them with bitter determination. "If you want me you'll have to come and get me!"

And then she turned and she ran!

With no clue as to where she was headed or even where she could find the exit, Berenice fled blindly through the catacombs. Her only consolation was that she could move faster than the two murderous revenants that pursued her so relentlessly, however, she was acutely aware that she would not be able to maintain this pace indefinitely.

Her directionless flight came to a faltering halt as she suddenly found herself within a chamber that had no other exits. It was a dead end and she was about to turn around and run back the way she had come when her foot knocked against something on the floor and she heard something metallic clatter against the stone.

Berenice looked down at her feet and saw that she was standing on the edge of a pentagram which had been scrawled across the floor in what looked and smelled like blood. Brass candlestick holders stood at each of the five points of the pentagram, except for at the point where Berenice stood; this was the metallic object that she had knocked over and it rolled around at her feet before coming to rest on a crack in the stone floor. Each of the candle wicks still carried the barest wisps of smoke drifting wraithlike into the air – they could only have been blown out fairly recently.

In the centre of the pentagram there was an ebony ceramic bowl that contained a congealing pool of what could only be blood. The discarded carcasses of three scrawny looking chickens lay around the bowl; their throats had been slit.

Berenice began to back out of the chamber. So many questions raced around inside her head.

Who could have done this? Was this what had brought the dead back to life? Why would somebody have done this?

The scraping footfalls of the revenants sounded behind her. Berenice spun round and saw them advancing down the tunnel towards her. There was no way now that she could run passed them.

She backed into the chamber until the wall was at her back and kept the torch shining ahead of her.

As the two homicidal corpses lurched into the chamber the torchlight picked that exact moment to flicker and die. Berenice screamed as she was plunged into oily, terrifying blackness. Rather redundantly she screwed up her eyes, crouching and cowering as low as she could and waited for the end to come.

The darkness was suddenly filled with a series of wet thudding noises accompanied by pitiful keening. Ultimately the keening stopped, but the wet thudding continued afterwards for, Berenice didn't know how long, but then even that went quiet. Then there was only an unnerving silence.

"Hello?" Berenice called into the darkness, her voice catching with the sobs of terror that still wracked her body.

A torchlight came on, but it was not her own.

A young man stood in the centre of the pentagram. He was holding a fireman's axe and its blade was covered with black ichor as was the face and clothes of her saviour. The dismembered remains of the revenants were strewn around at his feet.

It took a moment for Berenice to recognise the face beneath the gore.

"Pierre?" she whimpered, scarcely believing her good fortune.

Pierre put down the axe and walked over to her, holding out his hand. Berenice took it and allowed herself to be pulled to her feet.

"What the fuck is going on?" Pierre asked her. "What were those things?"

Berenice threw her arms around him and buried her face into his chest.

"Thank God for you, Pierre!" she wept. "If you had not come I don't know what would have happened."

Pierre encircled his arm around her and held her close. He kissed the top of her forehead.

"Do not worry, Berenice. Pierre is here now." He assured her. "Nothing can hurt you now."

She did not see the smug, self-satisfied smile that split his gore encrusted face as he led her away to find the exit.

12 Days Of Christmas 2016

12 Days Of Christmas 2016

Two Turtle Doves - Calum Chalmers

THE SNOWFALL OF FEATHERS trickled to the ground, claws swiped at beaks as blood splattered against the grass. Their bodies contorting, wrapping around one another as the feathered clumps fought for survival.

'Jimmy! Will you pay attention!'

The classroom erupted with laughter as Jimmy Haughton's gaze remained fixed out the window.

'Jimmy, I will not ask again'

Jimmy, hesitated a short while before turning to face Ms Denning's, her cruel face frozen in rage.

Picking up his pen he sighed as he turned to face the whiteboard. He wasn't going to apologise, he had nothing to apologise for! If Ms Denning's was good at her job she would be able to hold his attention; instead here he was daydreaming out the window while she twittered on about the times-table.

She had got some parts wrong, that's why Jimmy had lost interest, her inability to times 8 by 9 was her fault not his.

He gripped his pen tighter, infuriated by the brainless morons around him. Not one person noticed her error and they were all supposedly paying attention!

Closing his eyes and counting to ten, he swallowed hard, feeling the bile that had welled up in his throat slowly dissipate. He clicked the top of his pen; an imaginary nuclear explosion went off wiping the classroom out. Jimmy, protected by his superiority, watched as classmate after classmate burst into flames before crumbling into ashes.

He chuckled to himself before opening his eyes and catching the glare of Ms Denning's again.

'For fuck sake' he muttered under his breath before slouching back into his hard plastic chair and facing the front like a good little sheep.

Try as he might he couldn't shake the image of the cat fighting two birds, the detonation of their feathers each time his paw hit his mark, the frenzy as they each fought for their survival. He stole a glimpse out of the window only to see a pile of feathers being blown wistfully in the summer breeze.

There was no cat.

There were no birds.

Jimmy was up and out of his seat before the bell signalling the end of the day had finished ringing. By the time the shrill racket was reduced to a murmur Jimmy was out the door and heading towards the playing field. He could see the white pile before him and was eager to see who had won the battle.

As he neared he could see only a small splatter of blood, not enough to determine a victor, getting closer he could see no corpse, no avian chalk outline depicting the birds final resting place, no CSI Miami combing the scene for clues. Instead he found only feathers, no bird died today.

He looked into the tree and perched mere feet above him sat a disgruntled tabby cat, his skinny frame making it very clear that he had not managed to feed on any birds for quite some time.

Jimmy removed his lunch box from his rucksack and offered him a couple of cocktail sausages he had saved from his lunch. The moment he unclipped the box the cat was by his side purring in anticipation; Jimmy had made a new friend.

The following weeks Jimmy would head to the tree after school and meet with his friend; feeding him scraps of meat he had gathered throughout the day. A slither of meatloaf, a half-eaten burger, Jimmy presented a true feast each day. Over time their friendship grew and the cat, now named Andrew, would often follow Jimmy home and wait for Jimmy to emerge each morning.

Within a couple of months the cat was back to a healthy shape, his belly swung low and his fat little legs thundered along the pavement as he followed obediently behind Jimmy.

The only problem with Andrew's weight gain is that he became very lethargic; his ability to hunt birds had seeped away to nothing. Andrew would still watch the birds in the field but by the time he had struggled to his feet they had long gone. On one occasion Andrew mastered the art of camouflage and had successfully hidden himself in the undergrowth. However, as the birds neared his hiding place it was apparent that it was all too much and Andrew had fallen fast asleep.

In fact Jimmy had discovered that most cats in his neighbourhood were actually pretty shit at hunting birds. I mean seriously? How on Earth is a cat going to catch a bird that can fly away? How unfair was that! Something needed to be done, the birds had an unfair advantage and it seemed only Jimmy was aware.

That meant only one thing.

Jimmy had to find a way to give cats wings. But how?

He had read about a breed of Finch from the Galapagos that would evolve its beak depending on the food sources available. With each generation the beak would change to either pick food from the ground or from bushes, whichever was readily available. Perhaps he could trigger some form of evolutionary event which would allow cats to fly!

Full of a newfound purpose he scampered towards school in search of answers, there must be one science teacher who knows how to help.

Mr Caldock was busy scribbling formulas onto a scrap sheet of paper. His bushy beard dotted with the remains of his last few meals and his breath evidence that they weren't the most pleasant of feeds. Jimmy wasn't afraid of anyone but this man creeped him out something rotten. His bony little fingers, his penguin like waddle, that hunched over sneer that he exuded whenever something bad befell someone.

The older kids talked of a nervous breakdown, a once excellent mind that cured illnesses and sent men into space. But all that was too much, he became a recluse, took a job in a school and taught teenagers how magnets worked. Yes, this was the man who could help him.

Jimmy knocked on the door before stepping inside the classroom. Mr Caldock twisted his mouth into the most unsettling of smiles as he beckoned Jimmy closer.

As mentioned before Mr Caldock, as unpleasant as he was, wasn't actually scary. He had a fondness for the children and was always hugging them or encouraging the younger ones onto his knee. Being a boy Jimmy knew he had to watch his step; Mr Caldock seemed to only give boys after school detentions. It was as if he gave the girls much more leeway when they misbehaved. Jimmy always thought that was unfair but knew to keep his mouth shut, he didn't fancy detention, everyone always came home crying afterwards.

Jimmy, remembering to breathe through his mouth came close to the old man.

'Hello, young man, how may I help you?'

He leant in closer to Jimmy, an uncomfortable distance even if he wasn't so vile. A solitary hand came out to grip him tightly on the shoulder, his other nestled away under the desk.

'Mr Caldock…' he asked boldly.

'…How does one go about triggering an evolutionary event?'

Mr Caldock froze, his eyes locked on Jimmy as tiny little cogs seemed to whir away inside his mind.

After a few seconds Jimmy shifted on his feet, this movement seemingly kicking Mr Caldock back into gear.

'That is a very advanced question young man, something that requires a large amount of knowledge before you would even consider an answer'

Jimmy, unperturbed pushed on.

'Yes, well suppose someone had that knowledge or was at least willing to learn it, where would they go to get that answer?'

Mr Caldock sat back, his gaze still fixed on Jimmy.

'Well me of course'

Infuriated, Jimmy went to push Mr Caldock further, the man was old and dithery but surely he knew what Jimmy was getting at. However, before he could speak, Mr Caldock dropped a small notebook on the desk.

'And I suppose you would be the one who had or was willing to learn such knowledge?'

Jimmy stiffened in anticipation, the notebook sat mere inches from him, the answers he sought lay mere inches from his grasp. The small black leather book looked heavily worn; pages had been removed resulting in the spine being thicker than the book itself. White cracks spread across the body as the ancient leather split under years of use.

Mr Caldock, noticing Jimmy's excitement, opened the book.

Flicking through a couple of pages he hesitated before settling on a crisp unused page before gathering up a nearby pencil.

In thick, sturdy letters he wrote the words…

THEY ARE WATCHING

Jimmy took a few seconds to comprehend what he was reading; Mr Caldock's skeletal fingers shook softly as the pencil hovered above the page.

He continued.

LEAVE

His overgrown nose throbbed, blood rushed to his usually pale face as his hand began to shake wildly.

NOW

Jimmy gathered his bag and turned to face the door, whatever had frightened the old man wasn't going to frighten him. He spun back around, dropped his bag once more and faced Mr Caldock.

'No'

Mr Caldock's face didn't even flinch, he had prepared for this moment. Closing his book he stood up and left. Just as the door began to creak shut his, head popped back in urging Jimmy to follow him. Jimmy didn't waste a moment as he scurried after the old man.

12 Days Of Christmas 2016

'Next time I tell you to do something you do it, do I make myself clear?' With his voice full of rage his face remained a permanent sneer, Jimmy couldn't quite put the venom to the facial expression. Little did Jimmy know this was due to a massive stroke that was currently taking hold of Mr Caldock, his time with Jimmy was dwindling right before his eyes.

'I will tell you only once' (how true his words were) 'the answer you seek is found not far from here. The local library holds a small but very much perfect selection of books on the occult; in this section you need to find a book called the 'Incipientes Dirige Ad Malus Effercio'

Jimmy scribbled the name down as best he could.

'This book will tell you all you need to know and in a manner you will comprehend. However, when you take the book from the library 'They' will be informed'

'They? Who are 'They?' Jimmy felt a cold shiver run up his spine. He wasn't averse to breaking the rules but the manner in which Mr Caldock spoke of 'They' (or is it now 'Them') he couldn't help but feel worried.

'They are the Keepers of the Occult, the Guardians of the Dark, 'They' come from the shadows to ensure their secrets are kept safe'

'Is that who you warned me about earlier?' Jimmy couldn't stop his voice from trembling.

'The very same'

Jimmy pondered a while 'But if 'They' wanted it to remain a secret, why don't 'They' just take the book from the library and never return it?'

Mr Caldock's eyes widened, his mouth trembled with anticipation of an answer but no words seemed to materialise. A large amount of spit had formed in the corner of his mouth and was now trickling down his chin, Jimmy took a step back.

'Mr Caldock?' Jimmy's voice now a lacking in the confidence he had so previously mustered.

Jimmy took another step back, this one larger than the last. Was it 'Them'? Had 'They' hacked into his brain and wiped it of all his knowledge? Was Jimmy next!?

Mr Caldock fell forward landing face first on the pavement below, a small trickle of blood streamed into the gaps between the slabs as Mr Caldock's body slowly began to shut down. Jimmy never saw the blood; he never heard the guttural gurgling from the dying man's throat. Jimmy ran, he was already half way home by the time an ambulance was even called.

It wasn't until the next day after his Mother had got off the phone from school that he even knew Mr Caldock was actually dead. The janitor had found him, nothing he could have done; the stroke that befell Mr Caldock was far too catastrophic.

His Mother and Father explained the situation to him over breakfast, their constant smiles and occasional giggles reassured him that he was safe. The threat of 'Them' being pushed to the back of his mind with every spoonful of cereal. Well, not all the way back, just far enough to keep him on his toes; just far enough to keep 'Them' in his dreams at night.

The library was empty, as usual. A solitary librarian sat awkwardly on a backless stool, her plump little legs dangling a good foot from the ground. She didn't even turn to acknowledge Jimmy as he entered; instead she continued to tilt her mobile phone as she guided an animated Llama down a snow covered mountain.

Jimmy sneered, a whole building full of books, acres of new Worlds and knowledge and instead she sat pudgy eyed staring at a screen. He casually flicked her the finger as he walked past, needless to say it went unnoticed.

Roaming the towering shelves it didn't take long before he was standing before the Occult section, a mere 5 books propped up on the dusty shelf. Running his fingers along the spines he paused on a large leather-bound tome, the words 'Incipientes Dirige Ad Malus Effercio' written in eloquent golden scroll against a black backdrop.

The light above him flickered.

Swallowing hard he pulled the book from its home and headed to a nearby desk. Laying it down before him he drew a large breath and huffed a thick layer of dust from the cover, speckles of dirt tumbled through the air, spiralling into what Jimmy could have sworn was a figure of a bird, wings spread wide.

With a loud creak he pulled back the cover, the yellowing pages now on display, attached to the first was a small cardboard pocket with a library withdrawal card nestled inside. Slipping it from its sheath he fingered over the names, each one heavily scratched away. Through what he could discern there were 4 names, yet only one had any letters legible, S…N.

'Staan?' he pondered aloud.

Discarding the card he flicked onwards to the Contents; casting his finger down each chapter he soon stopped on one of interest;

Chapter 15:

Body Enhancement

A shudder of anticipation shot through his body like a firework traversing the night sky, he longed for the fantastic explosion to enlighten his brain.

The chapter was brief but very thorough. Jimmy, still a little unsettled by Mr Caldock's warning of 'They' (or 'Them' or whichever bloody tense he needed) had opted to copy every page into his notebook; if he didn't take the book out how would 'They' know he had read it. Satisfied with his deception he scribbled out every word and copied every picture. He took particular notice a section entitled tools required; most implements on the list seemed easy enough to liberate from the science lab but he seemed stumped by the requirement of Electrolytes.

'What the bastard are electrolytes?'

With closing time edging nearer and the very real risk that he could be locked in over the weekend, Jimmy opted to circle that word and research it further when he returned home. Completing his notes he carefully returned the book and made his way out of the building, once more extending his middle finger to the intolerable turd of a librarian that didn't fully appreciate her position in this wonderful building.

Despite Jimmy's eagerness to start the operation as soon as possible it had taken him a good month to steadily pilfer equipment from the school labs; one medical instrument at a time. The last thing he needed was the school to raise any concerns to 'They' (again, surely it should now be 'Them').

He had even managed to find a suitable source of electrolytes, several bottles of Lucozade. Although the amount of electrolytes was questionable, Jimmy had determined that 3 bottles should be more than enough for his needs.

Jimmy laid out his tools checking them off as he went,

Scalpel check

Forceps check

Scissors check

Tweezers check

Clips check

Needle and thread check

Superglue check

Lucozade check

Dressing check

Anaesthetic check

Car battery check

Happy he had all the equipment he needed he sat next to Andrew and softly patted his head, and now to find you your wings.

12 Days Of Christmas 2016

Early that very morning Jimmy had set a trap, a simple one but hopefully something with effect. He had snuck out and smothered the floor of the summerhouse with pitch, something he had learnt from Cinderella. Throwing a couple of handfuls of bread and seed into the centre he had left the door open and planned his return. Birds would often visit his garden; surely the promise of a free meal would be more than enough to entice them inside his little trap.

He stood by the back door eyes closed and holding the curtains shut, he could hear the flapping of wings, the coo from pigeons mixed in with the whistles and chirps of other various breeds. He could barely contain his excitement.

Yanking the curtains wide, revealing his prize like a daytime TV host, he stood before his marvellous bounty.

Now, there are some things you need to know about birds, some things that Jimmy didn't take into consideration.

1. Birds are very fragile creatures; they have very small hearts which mean that any undue stress or fear can result in a massive heart attack.

2. Birds shit, birds shit a lot. When you add in the fear from point 1 you end up with a lot of shit.

3. Birds are bastards; they don't care about the bird next to them. All they care about is surviving. Throw in some pitch and you have a clusterfuck of birds all scrambling amongst one another desperate to stay alive.

Now, imagine those 3 points and times that by say, 100 birds. That's right, Jimmy was faced with a massive twitching ball of angry/dead/terrified/shitting birds all stuck together as they fought for their freedom. Did I mention the shit? Surely I mentioned the shit; I mean there was a lot of it. The green and white slimy coating of excrement smothered every inch of the feathered pile.

Jimmy wretched.

Even Andrew wretched.

Jimmy grabbed the garden hose; faced with such carnage his brain focused on one task at a time, he needed to clean the birds off to see where to start unpicking.

Turning on the tap with a little too much enthusiasm, a jet of water shot out with frightening speed. The impact alone was enough to kill those unlucky enough to be hit by the torrent, the icy cold blast picking off the remaining few survivors. In less than 30 seconds Jimmy had killed every single bird.

Jimmy sobbed. Andrew sniffed the remains.

12 Days Of Christmas 2016

It took Jimmy most of the day to clear up the mess, the pitch clung to every inch of him.

Bastard Cinderella he mused, there is no way she would have only lost a shoe running down those stairs, should have ripped her flesh from her feet, he bitterly complained.

Adamant not to be defeated he resorted to plan B and ordered a bird online. He had stumbled across a local store that was able to order in a wide range of birds. Scrolling through the lists he ignored anything small, finches and budgies weren't going to cut it; Parrots were a good size but far too expensive, hawks were an interesting choice but the estimated delivery time was far too long.

Then he saw it, a beautiful Turtle Dove, its tabby wings a perfect match for Andrew! Straining to pick the obese feline up, Jimmy lifted Andrew to the screen allowing him to see his future wings; straining under the bulk Jimmy questioned, perhaps a second pair of wings would be beneficial.

Jimmy quickly updated his order to two turtle doves.

Finally the day had come, Jimmy had collected his birds from the store and being a caring soul he had given them one last feast before they made their sacrifice.

12 Days Of Christmas 2016

Once more he ran through his checklist (now complete with birds) before shaving the fur from Andrews back. The cat was surprisingly willing, purring with each stroke of the blade, perhaps aware that soon he would be given the gift of flight.

Opening the travel case on the nearby table his two birds stood before him, their beady eyes darting around monitoring their new surroundings. Jimmy gently picked up each one and placed them into a waiting plastic box before sealing the lid. A quick twist of a nozzle and the nitrous oxide began to hiss into the box, the birds, intrigued by the new noise headed face first towards their impending death.

Finally he was ready to start his surgery, giving the flightless Andrew one last kiss he started to administer the Anaesthetic.

Soon you will be free to fly amongst the birds; soon you will rule the skies. Jimmy wiped a solitary tear from his eye as his friend slipped into unconsciousness.

Jimmy had opted for a low level of anaesthetic, this was his first operation and he didn't want to lose his friend through a miscalculation. However, the low concentration meant he had only a short time to complete his task. Jimmy wasted no time in starting his incisions; carefully cutting down the spine, he delicately peeled back a layer of skin to reveal the muscle below.

Turning to a veterinary manual he made one last check before noting the correct muscle to slice into. With expert precision he opened the meaty red chunk and lay down his tools. At this point he recalled surgeons would wipe their brow and exhale sharply, keen to act like a professional he too performed this ritual, inadvertently smearing blood across his forehead in the process.

He unclipped the lid of the box to his side and lifted the lifeless bodies of the two turtle doves who had nestled in the corner, their bodies still warm, just as required.

Holding them together he noticed one was ever so slightly larger than the other, it was the larger of the two he decided to work on first. Spreading the wings he clipped the tips to his workbench; taking a fresh scalpel he carved down what he deemed the shoulder of the bird, tracing his blade down into the 'armpit' (in this instance however he thought it pertinent to refer to it as the 'wingpit', it seemed right to use proper wording during such delicate work.)

The wing came away from the main body with surprising ease. Jimmy continued his work until four wings were laid out before him, each one clipped open to a full spread. The bodies were unceremoniously placed on the floor by his feet; he made a mental note that if he ever needed to do this work again he would be sure to have a bin to hand.

Now the hard part, Jimmy took one of the larger wings and made note of ensuring he was attaching it to the correct side. Spreading the wing muscle into Andrews's incision he carefully stitched the wing to his friends back muscle. Returning to his wing stockpile he continued his task until all four were sewn into place. He washed over the surgery with a bottle of water, checking that every stitch was tight and in the correct place.

Now for the secret ingredient, electrolytes.

Jimmy emptied all three bottles of Lucozade over the open skin making sure that the freshly stitched area was suitably coated; he softly rubbed the muscles making sure they absorbed the electrolytey goodness.

With one eye on the clock he knew he was running out of time, in less than 10 minutes Andrew would be awake. Grabbing the car battery he hurriedly connected the clips.

Nothing, not even a flicker of movement.

He checked the connections, sparked the clips to ensure there was a charge but still nothing occurred. What am I missing? He pondered aloud. He had followed the book to its every word; he had read, re-read and even re-re-read every passage until it was etched on his brain. Yet it hadn't work, his whole experiment was deemed a disastrous failure.

He stitched the loose flaps of flesh back into place; Andrew was due to wake at any minute and the last thing Jimmy wanted was a skinless cat tearing around the neighbourhood with 4 dead wings attached. 'They' would become suspicious. No, a half operated on cat would raise too many eyebrows and raise even more questions, questions Jimmy wouldn't have the answers for.

By the time Jimmy snipped off the last stitch Andrews whiskers had started to twitch. Soon his eyes were open; blinking as they tried to shake off the drug induced haze that was still working its way out of his system. Swaddling his wings in a bandage, Jimmy noticed a slight trembling in the wings as if something was rustling beneath them. Maybe all was not lost? Maybe there was hope after all? With his heart filled of renewed hope he deposited Andrew in a large cage allowing him to rest in peace. It would be a few days before he would be steady enough to try his wings out. Jimmy could hardly wait. Andrew was indifferent.

The day had finally arrived, the stitches were healing nicely and the occasional quaking from the wings under the bandage had Jimmy skipping with excitement. He was positive that his work had been a success, now all he needed to know is if the 4 wings had been enough to lift Andrews's hefty size.

12 Days Of Christmas 2016

Andrew was busy sniffing his mother's flower bed; Jimmy knew that his excitement was buried deep, deep down, but as soon as the dressing was removed he would see the true joy in his friend's eyes.

Jimmy cut through the bandage with great care, after all this time he couldn't risk clipping Andrews's wings, Jimmy wasn't even sure if they would grow back. But, if the surgery was a success he had no issue with replacing his wings on a regular basis, a sort of service every couple of months, anything for his friend.

As soon as the last slice was made the wings burst out of the dressing as if they had a life of their own, each feather spread wide like fingers on a hand (albeit many more fingers and with more feather than the average human hand). Andrew, startled by the commotion so close to him, sprinted away; even with his girth he managed a decent speed as he hurtled towards the shed.

The wings, tickled by the wind running through them began to flap. At first they moved individually, shifting Andrew side to side as they searched for their rhythm. The unrelenting movement continued to surprise Andrew who was now running laps around Jimmy's Father's pond. Jimmy, close behind, was desperate to calm his friend but couldn't risk grabbing the delicate wings, instead he flapped wildly about the garden chasing Andrew which only added to the ongoing mayhem.

Andrew was easily at his top speed by the time the wings found their tempo, and with the wings doing what they do best it wasn't long before Andrews pudgy little legs were pumping away about 3 inches off the ground. Soon he was a good foot off the ground with his legs continuing to whir; it wasn't until he was skimming the shed roof that Andrew realised he was flying.

Jimmy meanwhile, was jumping with excitement, his hands pumping into the air like a 80s rom-com credit reel. It had worked; he had given the gift of flight to a cat, a freaking cat! He couldn't wait for Andrew to sneak up on his first victim, to see that bird with its smug, beady little eyes as it starts its ascent, only to find Andrew launch himself into the skies to pursue it.

Andrew had continued to circle the garden, his feet now hanging limp as his wings took over. His fearful face scanning the ground below him as he rose even higher, the repeated circuits now taking their toll on his stomach, it wouldn't be long until he had to vomit.

His wings pumped harder, finding the strength to push further to their limits. Andrew was now clear of the chimney, a full two stories above the ground and continuing. It was only at this point did Jimmy realise something was wrong.

Andrews's rotations arced wider; at this height Jimmy wasn't entirely sure if he could make out the feline retching, only when a globule of vomit landed by his side was he sure.

Something was wrong…Andrew couldn't control the wings! He was merely being lifted by them! The longer he remained in flight, the stronger the wings were getting; and the stronger the wings got the quicker Andrew was rising. Jimmy struggled to make out Andrew, the brown dot circling the entire neighbourhood. He began to panic, he could do nothing but watch as his friend headed skyward.

Andrew was now looking down on the whole town. He could make out the school where he first met Jimmy, the tree that they would have lunch under, even the bushes he had to sleep under before Jimmy found him. He longed for those days back, he longed for Jimmy, most of all though, he longed for the ground.

By now the wings began to tire, each flap became harder than the last and with it their ferocity was depleting. Andrew, now truly fed up of his ordeal saw the opportunity to strike; he flicked up his back leg and scratched at the wings. Claws dug into the feathers, tearing them from their roots. The wings now too weak to fight back gave into their attack, now drooping to his side.

12 Days Of Christmas 2016

Andrew continued his onslaught; he had disabled one and was close to uprooting another.

He began to descend.

Jimmy watched in horror as a flurry of feathers detonated above Andrew. From his viewpoint he couldn't make out what was really happening but new that it was going to end badly. He scoured the garden for something to break his friends fall. Only last year his parents offered to buy him a trampoline for his birthday. Why didn't he take them up on their offer? Why couldn't he be a normal kid with normal childish desires? No, he opted for an antique dentist set.

Time was running out and all Jimmy managed to find was the net his Father used to cover the pond. He quickly tied it off on the gardens fence posts and ensured it was tight enough to break Andrews fall. Hopefully Andrew will see the target and will do something, anything, to aim for it.

Andrew however didn't have time to aim.

One final kick and the third wing was off, the forth now flapped wildly above him; although not on its own accord.

Andrew was falling and at a horrendous rate, he began to tumble mid-air, he caught a glimpse of the school, then a tree, Jimmy's roof, and then nothing. Andrew lay motionless on the patio.

Falling to his knees Jimmy howled like a barbarian heading into battle, his hands gripping his hair almost tearing them from their roots.

What have I done? WHAT HAVE I DONE!?

He felt his throat nearly tear with the ferocity of his screams, his lungs burned as the ashes from his exploding heart filled every crevice. How could he have been so foolish? How could he have risked his dear friend's life? Jimmy wept on the floor, his sleeves dripping with mucus as his emotions flowed from his nose.

He crawled over to the remains of his friend and cradled them like an infant. Andrews tongue hung listlessly from his mouth, a small slither of blood trickled from his nose; his wings now nothing but bloody stumps. Jimmy embraced his cat, rocking as his hand stroked lightly down his side.

He sat there until nightfall and then sat some more. Dawn came and went, lunches were missed, but he didn't leave his friends side.

It takes a few days for cats to reach the next of their available 9 lives….

A Partridge In A Pear Tree - Matthew Cash

HE KNEW IT WAS wrong but he couldn't help himself. She was the prettiest girl he had ever seen in his life.

When the Dawson family moved into the house next door he had been apprehensive like any normal person would be at the news of a new family. There had been mention of children when the man had arrived with his wife to view the house.

He hated children, unruly noisy brats, judging by how old the man and woman had appeared the kids were probably toddlers. That was all he needed.

Their gardens were separated by a partial fence and a colossal tree that spread its two thick lower branches outwards like a holy man singing hosanna. Other branches spread over both their properties equally. The tree was ancient, several hundred years old, and was one of the biggest fruit trees around.

When he watched the Dawsons view the expanse of grass he could already see the expression of excitement on Mr Dawson's face when he eyed that stretched out branch.

Perfect for a swing. That's what Peter predicted he was thinking, it was a natural thing to do, the family who lived there before had done the same.

Peter was perched in his usual place, on the arm of a green sofa, the padding moulded to the shape of his buttocks from hours sat in the same place being a nosy parker.

The Dawsons' car had turned up behind the removal van and the mother and father got out followed by a sandy haired boy of about nine or ten. Peter was pleased as this hopefully meant he was past his screaming toddler days. The far side rear door opened, Peter expected a younger child, and a surprise burst of autumnal red hair made him jump from the sofa and prize apart the slat blinds for a better look.

A tall girl had gotten out of the car, stretching out her arms and legs as she surveyed the house. She was a lot taller than her mother, like her father, and had a headful of ginger hair which fell down her lumberjack shirt like a lion's mane. It was hard for him to determine her age from this far away but her womanly figure and big firm breasts that pushed against her shirt made it impossible for him to care how old she was.

She laughed silently at something Mr Dawson said, her red locks shaking as she held a hand over a big, wide mouthed grin.

12 Days Of Christmas 2016

Peter was spellbound. It was love at first sight for him, never before in his fifty years on this planet had anyone else had such an effect on him. Within thirty seconds of laying his eyes on her his pants and trousers were around his ankles and his fist pumping up and down his erection as though his life depended on it.

After he sprayed the dust heavy net curtains with his clumpy spunk and wiped himself on the lacey fabric he covered himself up and thought about taking them a housewarming present.

Greg Dawson sat down heavily into the armchair without removing the plastic anti-dust blanket. He was knackered, all the heavy lifting was done, the removal men paid and gone, all boxes in their allocated rooms. The evening sun bled through the magnificent pear tree's branches outside painting a woodland mural on the lounge walls. A scattering of the tear drop shaped fruits lay on the grass surrounding the tree in various states of rot. Greg smiled however, the weather was nice and it would give him and Davey something to do outside whilst the girls sorted out indoors. Then after the garden was sorted he would go to the hardware store and see what he needed for rigging up a swing on that thick old branch. If it were strong enough that is.

"It's lovely isn't it?" Faye Dawson said as she fell across his lap, two bottles of lager in her hands. She was a short woman with cropped red hair the same shade as her daughter's.

Greg accepted the cold bottle from his wife and nodded as he sipped the beer. "We've struck lucky with this one."

"Oh and before you ask, Davey is zonked out on his bed and Val's sorting out her essentials."

Greg smirked, "where to plug her spaghetti mess of chargers I suppose."

Faye laughed, "You guessed right."

Greg kissed his wife on the mouth, both their lips wet with beer." I love you."

"I love you too and I've ordered Chinese."

Greg cheered, "now I love you even more."

The doorbell rang and Greg looked at his wife, "is that them now?"

"I doubt it, I only got off the phone just before I came in." Faye jumped off her husband, placed the beer bottle on the unpacked coffee table and went to answer the door.

Val nearly beat her too it as she jogged down the stairs in a vest and shorts, clunky headphones wrapped around her neck like jewellery.

Faye answered the door and smiled politely at the man standing there. He shuffled about nervously, a bag in his hand.

"Hi," Faye said warmly, Val smiled awkwardly over her shoulder the smile fading when she saw the man's dark eyes flit over her exposed skin.

The man cleared his throat and smoothed back an overlong dark grey fringe from his eyes. "Hello, I'm Peter, your neighbour."

Faye shook his hand and tried not to let the disgust of its moisture show on her face. "Oh hi, I'm Faye and this is my daughter Val, that's short for Valentina."

Peter smiled with the bashfulness of an adolescent and muttered 'Valentina' like he was trying the word for size.

Val frowned, stuck her thumb up and trotted back up the stairs.

Faye worriedly noticed Peter's eyes follow her daughter up the stairs, "Then we have my husband Greg and son Davey who I'm sure you'll meet soon enough."

Peter turned his attention back to Faye and offered her the bag he held.

Faye took it apprehensively and saw it was filled with pears.

"I picked the best ones from my side as I knew the ones on your's wouldn't be any good now. They've been sat there too long." He licked his lips nervously, eyes flicking from Faye to the stairs behind her. "Rotting."

Faye scrunched her face up and smiled uncomfortably, one hand held the bag as the other gently started to push the door closed. "Well it's been lovely to meet you but we have so much to do as I'm sure you can imagine."

Peter shook his head, shaking away his trance, "Yes yes yes. Lots to do, busy busy." He paused. "I have to finish making my pear compote to put in my pies."

"Oh lovely," Faye said with fake enthusiasm inching the door closed even more.

Peter's fingers fluttered over his mouth in a comical thinking gesture, "I could maybe bring you and Valentina one when I've made them."

Faye noticed his dirty hands, fingernails gnarly and yellow, "the fruit is just fine, we both have an allergy to..." Faye searched the confines of her brain for something relevant but all that came out was, "pie crust."

Peter nodded and turned around and walked away without a farewell.

12 Days Of Christmas 2016

Faye shut the door and heard dry laughter coming from the top of the stairs. Val sat out of sight of the door but eavesdropping on her mother's friendly chat with the next door neighbour. "we're allergic to pie crust?"

Faye screwed her mouth up to stifle a laugh just in case the man could hear.

"Allergic to freaky perverts with no personal hygiene more like." Val said picking at a scab on her knee.

Faye winced at her daughter's words, mostly because she thought them true, "I'm sure he's okay really, probably just lonely."

Val shrugged and jumped up, "so are most serial killers. I bet he's got his mother to keep him company, although she's probably been dead decades."

Faye let out a hoot of laughter and went off to finish her beer.

He couldn't believe his luck that night. The Dawsons' house was a mirror opposite of his with the two main large bedrooms adjacent to one another. He presumed the parents would have that room but no. Peter sat in the dark of his parents' bedroom watching the house opposite, watching the bedroom opposite.

12 Days Of Christmas 2016

He watched as Valentina sat on her bed staring at some electronic screen held in her hand, one leg stretched out and the other bent, knee pointing towards the ceiling, toes curled beneath the other knee.

Her skin was like porcelain, so pale, it made the contrast between her big pink mouth and hot hair the more starker. She was divine.

Peter smiled at her and wished himself beside her, fingertips brushing that smooth white flesh.

It was dark outside now too. No nearby streetlights meant that the gardens were pitch black at night unless the moon was out.

A cool breeze slipped through the window and he crept forward to shut it.

That was when he noticed the two thick branches of the tree. It was like it was preordained. Each branch ended a few feet below the two houses main bedroom windows. He had never thought about it before even though the tree had been there all his life.

The branch could be easily reached from his window and just beneath Valentina's, above the patio doors of their lounge, the other branch ended with a thick V which was covered by the overhanging leaves.

A perfect place to hide.

12 Days Of Christmas 2016

Peter sat at the foot of his parents' bed, careful not to disturb them, pulled down his trousers and pants and continued to stare at Valentina.

"Aw man, but I kinda like the sun shining in on me in the morning." Val whined as she watched her mother hanging curtains up at her window.

"You're eighteen years old and we live opposite the house of someone who you yesterday insinuated was a modern Norman Bates. I'm not going to give him the opportunity to watch you get undressed."

Val rolled across the bed, "I always get changed and stuff in the bathroom anyway, especially with the little Shit running around."

Faye cast her a disapproving look, "I wish you wouldn't call your brother that. Come and help me with these."

Peter nestled against the gigantic dark brown breast of his mother and used both hands to lift the other towards his face. He latched onto the elongated black nipple like a hungry baby and sucked greedily. The milk was good but not that plentiful and he had sucked her dry in under a minute. He pulled her tit from his mouth and made a sad face as he looked at her big round, tear-stained face.

There was residue of vomit on the cloth he had used to gag her with.

Peter didn't want his mother to choke to death so he untied the gag. His mother spat out a torrent of sick that had collected in her mouth and began to cry, "Please, please let us go, we aren't your parents."

Peter smiled and put the gag back on. He rolled over and smiled at the comatose figure of a decrepit skeleton of a man, his mouth was a puckered O as he sucked air in through a toothless mouth ready to expel in a grunting snore.

The big naked black woman groaned as Peter crawled over naked body and stood at the side of the bed. The restraints still bound her tightly, that was good.

He patted her sweat coated shoulder, "Daddy will be awake soon and you know what he's like when he wakes up." Peter chuckled as he peeked down at his own erection which stood up proudly. "He's just like me."

12 Days Of Christmas 2016

Davey stuck a triangle of toast in his mouth as he ran through the kitchen. Faye opened her mouth to say something when Davey pointed at the television set. "Ha, he looks like a zombie." Before continuing out of the back door.

Faye glimpsed the news article whilst tidying up the breakfast things.

A large buxom African lady and the ninety year old man who was in her care at the time had been abducted the previous afternoon in the park by someone who pretended to be a taxi driver.

Faye wondered why the hell anyone would do such a thing.

Peter gritted his teeth as he strained with the effort of moving his mother's arm to attach the restraints to the bedposts.

"Mother," he wheezed as he dug a foot into the side of her bosom to give himself leverage for moving her arm. "Stop fighting."

Sweat soaked and panting he fastened the handcuffs to the bed post and breathed a huge sigh of relief. He smiled down at his mother's big chocolate skinned body stretched out in a star on the filthy bed. She really was an amazing woman, she did so much for him.

Ignoring her cries of disgust through the gag he moved to the comatose ninety year old figure of his dad. "Hey Daddy, Mummy's been waiting for you." Peter said huffing as he yanked down the piss and shit stained pyjama bottoms of the old man.

Once he had stripped the old man off he manoeuvred him about like a man-sized rag doll, grabbed him under the arms, hands laced across his chest. He hefted the man, even though he barely weighed much more than seven stone, and flopped him down on top of his mother.

The virtually lifeless body of the man just lay on top of the enormous woman.

Peter walked around the bed checking everything was right. "Physical intimacy is important in healthy relationships. You don't want to end up getting a divorce do you?"

Mother screwed her eyes shut grimacing and turned her face away as a long line of drool spilled from the old man's mouth and the sudden warmth that trickled down her thigh told her that he had wet himself.

Peter crouched down to where his father's boney hips rested between the colossal thighs of his mother. "Come on Daddy," he said encouragingly and reached out a hand and jiggled his father's clammy sagging testicles. No reaction at all.

Peter swore and paced the room, sex was an important part in marital relationships.

Something caught his eye out the window and he temporarily forgot his situation.

Valentina sat on the grass in the sun, in a bikini top and shorts. It took all of his will power not to press his face up against the glass. The paleness of her skin, the red swatches of material cupping her ripe breasts, it was too much, too hard to resist.

Peter stared really hard at her, mentally recording the image before turning to his parents. "Okay Daddy, I'll help you out this once." He grinned sheepishly and removed his own clothes.

He crawled up the bed and knelt between his mother and father's legs. He grabbed his father by the hips and shoved his body further up his mother's. "Now you just give Daddy lots of big kisses Mummy, you're both going to enjoy this." Peter said poking his head around his father's waist and winking.

Peter smiled when he saw how wet his mother and the bed was, she was really excited bless her. He moved closer, his erection poised before his mother's vagina. He closed his eyes and pictured Valentina before thrusting into his mother's hot wet gash.

"Well, what do you think?" Greg said waving a hand towards the swing he had hung from the thick branch.

"Will it hold?" Faye said with uncertainty.

Greg sat on the wooden slat that was used for the seat and swung back and forth. "Weeeee."

"Dad, you're such a kid." Val chuckled in embarrassment as she sat up on one elbow.

Greg stuck his tongue out and kicked one of his flip-flops off his foot in her direction.

Val narrowly dodged the flying missile and rolled onto her front laughing.

A loud war cry came from the house as Davey leapt out of the back door with the world's largest water pistol.

The Dawsons ducked and dived and ran about chasing one another, having fun in their new garden. They had never been happier.

Excited giggling made Peter run to the window. Valentina chasing her brother, soaking wet, a fake evil grin on her face as she ran after him squirting him with a big water gun. She looked even better wet. Peter knew that he must have her completely. Tonight he would use the tree to get to her room. She would be worth it, even if he only had contact for a minute and her dad pounced on him, it would be worth it.

He scowled at his parents' bed. Something was wrong with father, he lay on the floor still, his head pointing the wrong way and his chest had stopped going up and down a while ago.

Mother was ill too. He had done a bad thing when he had unzipped her middle with the bread knife. There was mess everywhere, reds and browns mostly but even though it was a bit yucky he kinda thought it was pretty.

Peter sighed with lovesick affection at his love, his valentine, Valentina, and then back at his mother's unzipped stomach.

I wonder, he thought, if father could fit in there?

He stood up and tilted his head as he thought about whether it would be possible. "If I can get rid of all the yucky stuff and then use Mummy's sewing kit, then I think it will work." He clapped his hands together excitedly like a child, "Then you and Daddy will be together forever." Peter's smile vanished and was replaced with something more sinister, "I'm a big boy now, it's time for you to get your own place now. I'm moving my girlfriend Valentina in tonight."

12 Days Of Christmas 2016

Greg collapsed into the armchair and sat staring out through the patio doors at the setting sun. He was bushed, another busy day but it had been so much fun. Faye lay snoozing on the settee, the day of sorting out the house and fun in the sun had taken its toll on her. But again another country's cuisine had been driven to them speedily to save her the added hassle of preparing a family meal.

They would go grocery shopping the next day, Greg planned their first of many epic BBQS. He would go and invite their weird ass neighbour later on, partly to be neighbourly, partly to make sure he knew he could kick the shit out of him if he caught him sleazing up his daughter.

A beer in one hand, a belly full of Mexican food, Greg smirked and risked resting his eyes for a few minutes.

Peter let go of the sheet after it had settled on top of his parents. Movement from the room opposite caught his attention and he pounced to the net curtains. His heart started pounding at the quick glimpse he had seen between the gap in Valentina's curtains. Long wet red hair, a bath towel wrapped around her chest. She pressed a button on something and rock music blared out of unseen speakers.

Desire burned through him and at that very moment he knew he would risk everything to have her.

12 Days Of Christmas 2016

The night was as dark as it was going to get, her's was the only light on in the house. It was now or never.

Peter climbed out of the window and lowered himself carefully to the branch.

"Huh what?" Greg said head snapping up as Faye woke him.

"Let's go to bed." She said from the dark lounge.

He stood up groggily, "You go on up, it's still early. I'm just gonna pop round to that weirdos and invite him to the BBQ tomorrow."

Faye groaned but kissed him on the cheek and left the room.

The night was so hot, he wished he had left his shirt off. Peter crawled along the branch on his belly down towards the trunk of the tree. The light from Valentina's window was like a beacon to him, beckoning him over, giving him the strength to perform this dangerous task. A whirr of a hairdryer came from her open window, Peter clung to the branch and leant out slightly for a better view.

In those luxurious four inches of curtain gap he could see Valentina drying her beautiful red locks, the black bath towel had slipped down and her back was unveiled.

He saw a row of little black splodges which he presumed were tattoos running down her spine. He wanted to kiss them.

He felt himself stiffen as he peeped on his love so he sped up his crawling.

He hugged the tree trunk and moved onto the branch over the Dawson's side.

Greg banged on the door and thought it was in serious need of replacing. The wood was old, paint flaking, a little metal plaque screwed to the door was almost completely rusted over. Greg picked at the plaque and took his phone out to read the engraving. Mr and Mrs Partridge. He giggled to himself and tried to remember what Faye had said the guy's name was. Paul, Patrick, no Peter. Peter Partridge, sounded like Spiderman or some shit.

Greg knocked even louder and the door opened inwards.

Peter wrapped an arm around the branch and hid in the V that tapered off into a shower of leaves that he felt sure would obscure him. He was so close to her window if he reached out he could touch it.

12 Days Of Christmas 2016

He knew what he planned to do, simply climb in through the open window and have her.

But Valentina did something that nearly made him fall from the tree. She turned towards the window fully naked.

Peter let out a gasp that she would have heard if it wasn't for the music. There was no way he could pass on this opportunity. Holding on to the branch tightly with one arm he pulled down his trousers and pants and freed his painful erection.

He caressed the shaft of his penis as he drank in every detail of her perfect young body. There was no way he could stop himself now. A cool breeze lapped around his hot penis and tickled his sweaty balls.

"Oh my God," Peter whispered feeling himself rise to what felt like it would be one hell of an orgasm, "I've gotta touch my balls, I've gotta touch my balls."

He increased the yanking of his dick and balanced himself in the V. He had to come whilst looking at her nudity, he had too.

"I've got to touch my balls." Peter whispered one last time and let go of the branch to cup the pendulous swinging orbs.

12 Days Of Christmas 2016

Greg was about to enter the neighbour's house when he heard an almighty crack come from his back garden.

He turned and ran towards his house as lights started coming on throughout the building. As he ran across the lawn towards the back of the house the light from the lounge shone on the pear tree. The branch which he had hung the swing off had snapped completely and crashed through the patio doors.

He raced through the backdoor, his heart pounding when he heard his wife screaming loudly. Oh Jesus, don't let anyone be hurt, he prayed to whoever as he fumbled with the back door with visions of Val or Davey impaled on a splintered tree limb.

The sight in the lounge blew him away. The branch had ploughed into the lounge obliterating the patio doors, overturning the sofa and killing the flat screen television. If anyone had been in the room they would have been seriously hurt.

Luckily none of his family had been, but hanging in the middle of the room like some bizarre light fitting was Peter the next door neighbour. His face was wedged into the V of the branch, neck stretched out too far, broken obviously, a deep laceration, probably from contact with the patio doors, had opened up his abdomen spilling his guts onto the new carpet. His feet danced so madly that the pants and trousers which were hanging round them dropped off onto the steaming innards on the floor. At eye level with his wife Peter's erection wilted like a deflating balloon as he died.

The surprise that was found in the Dawsons' lounge was nothing compared with the surprise parcel that the police found in Peter's parents bed.

Author Biographies

Calum Chalmers

Calum Chalmers hates anything nice, in particular he loathes happiness; so writing horror kinda works out for him.
If his darkness excites you then check out his story 'The Change' featured in Thirteen Tales of Therianthropy and 'Cosmic Unicorn Thunderfuck' featured in Unicornado; to just name a few (he has more, I promise)

C L Raven:

C L Raven are identical twins from Cardiff who love all things horror. They spend their time looking after their animal army and drinking more Red Bull than the recommended government guidelines. They write short stories, novels and articles for Haunted Magazine and have been published in various anthologies and horror magazines. They've been longlisted in the Exeter Novel Prize twice, the Flash 500 Novel competition and the Bath Novel Award. Soul Asylum was shortlisted in the 2012 National Self-Publishing Awards and Deadly Reflections was highly recommended in the 2014 awards. Several short stories have also been long and shortlisted in various competitions. Their most recent publication was in the Mammoth Book of Jack the Ripper, which makes their fascination with him seem less creepy. Along with their friend Neen, they prowl the country hunting for ghosts for their YouTube show, Calamityville Horror and can also be found urb-exing in places they shouldn't be. Every Friday night, they can be found playing D&D/RPGs with their group, Disaster Class, which always ends in failing dice rolls and derailing all the DM's plans. Sorry Tom.

Links: Blog – clraven.wordpress.com

Twitter - @clraven @calamityhorror

Facebook - www.facebook.com/pages/CL-Raven-Fanclub

https://www.facebook.com/CatsTalesOfTerror?ref=hl

Instagram – clraven666 CalamityvilleHorror666

Edward Breen:

Edward Breen is a Kent based writer, husband and father to three cats and a human child. He loves horror and fantasy and writes short stories mainly. One of his many manuscripts will, hopefully, become a novel some day, but for now you can catch him at https://dwreadswriting.blogspot.co.uk as well as on Facebook @Edward Breen.

Betty Breen:

Betty Breen writes because she must and loves doing it. New to the world of writing this is her first publication (of many). A creative a heart, watch this space for more from this new entry into the Horror sphere. Catch her on Twitter @just_betty5

Ezekiel Jacobs:

Whilst frequenting the purveyors of the finest cuisine Manchester had to offer I was bewildered to find my taste buds quiver with a new and as yet unexperienced craving - tacos made from the skin and flesh of the mentally ill.

I stumbled into a specialist in this delicacy, a vendor by the name of Taco Hell.

Their highly illegal but eagerly sought after snack - wacos- as they amusingly entitled them were every bit as disgusting as I imagined, and no sooner had I finished my fifth one, with a willy con carne filling, I felt the urge to vomit.

I spotted their dumpster, overflowing with the bits that didn't go in the mincer. I lifted the lid and let out a screaming hot geyser of gruel. This geyser landed on a geezer who was hunched up in the dumpster, emaciated, completely naked and drawing strange hieroglyphs onto the filthy walls of the bin using the decapitated corpse of a chicken. Amongst the rancid odour and detritus I noticed a few coherent words within the neanderthal cave painting . Along with the spasticated hieroglyphics, which I translated using Google, I added these snippets of English and produced the tale you have read.

I coaxed the shivering naked Ezekiel with a box of After Eights and a Razzle magazine and he now safely lives in my coat cupboard with the corpse of my first wife and the entrance to Narnia

Daryl Lewis Duncan:

Daryl comes from a small town in Northern Ireland where he lives with his wife and two boys. He is part of a small amateur production team called Dead On Films who released their first film last year entitled 'Vapours'. He is a massive fan of horror literature and recently self-published his own zombie novella called 'Skud'. He is currently working on a vampire script based in Northern Ireland to be filmed in the Spring and is involved in a few horror anthologies in the coming year.

12 Days Of Christmas 2016

Mark Leney And Forbes King:

Mark Leney is from the UK and lives and writes in Bromley with his wife Nicola and his daughter Sacha.

They did used to have goldfish, but they have since been replaced by robots.

Mark looks forward to the day when wolves and dragons become a viable option as a household pet.

Forbes King is a writer from the deep south, no think deeper than that, yes, that's write, no, that's right from New Zealand and he specializes in fantasy and dabbles in other genres from time to time. He lives with the many voices in his head telling him to stop what he's doing and write and so he does that...

Jessica McHugh:

Jessica McHugh is a novelist, poet, and internationally produced playwright running amok in the fields of horror, sci-fi, young adult, and wherever else her peculiar mind leads. She's had eighteen books published in seven years, including her bizarro romp, "The Green Kangaroos," her

Post Mortem Press bestseller, "Rabbits in the Garden," and her edgy YA series, "The Darla Decker Diaries." More information on her published and forthcoming fiction can be found at JessicaMcHughBooks.com.

FB: http://www.facebook.com/author.JessicaMcHugh

Twitter: @theJessMcHugh

IG: @theJessMcHugh

Anthony Cowin:

Anthony Cowin writes dark and twisted tales that have been published in many print anthologies, chapbooks, magazines and e-zines. He's currently writing a dystopian sci-fi novel and editing for publishers and independent writers. You can connect on Twitter at @TonyCowin or visit his website www.anthonycowin.com

Matthew Cash:

Matthew Cash, or Matty-Bob Cash as he is known to most, was born and raised in in Suffolk; which is the setting for his debut novel Pinprick. He is compiler and editor of Death By Chocolate, a chocoholic horror anthology, and the 12Days Anthology, and has numerous releases on Kindle and several collections in paperback.

He has always written stories since he first learnt to write and most, although not all, tend to slip into the many layered murky depths of the Horror genre.

His influences ranged from when he first started reading to Present day are, to name but a small select few; Roald Dahl, James Herbert, Clive Barker, Stephen King, Stephen Laws, and more recently he enjoys Adam Nevill, F.R Tallis, Michael Bray, Gary Fry, William Meikle and Iain Rob Wright (who featured Matty-Bob in his famous A-Z of Horror title M is For Matty-Bob, plus Matthew wrote his own version of events which was included as a bonus).

He is a father of two, a husband of one and a zoo keeper of numerous fur babies.

You can find him here:

www.facebook.com/pinprickbymatthewcash

https://www.amazon.co.uk/-/e/B010MQTWKK

12 Days Of Christmas 2016

Printed in Great Britain
by Amazon